MY FRIEND SANCHO

MY FRIEND
SANCHO

Amit Varma

First published in 2009 by Hachette India
An Hachette UK company

2

ISBN: 978-81-906173-1-4

Hachette India
612/614 (6th Floor), Time Tower,
MG Road, Sector 28, Gurgaon-122001, India

Typeset in Bodoni MT 12/17.5 by
Mindways Design, New Delhi

Printed in India by
Gopsons Papers Ltd, Noida

To Jasmine
With love and gratitude

1. Man Bites Dog

Headline: Man Swats Himself to Death

Strap: Byculla Carpenter Tries to Crush Mosquito on His Stomach, Kills Himself Instead

Copy: The persistent buzz of a mosquito can get so frustrating sometimes that one is driven to violence. That's what happened yesterday to Sunil Shettigar, a carpenter in Byculla. Shettigar was sitting on a bench waiting for a train at Byculla station when a pesky mosquito started bothering him. He saw it land on his stomach and gave it one mighty blow. He then collapsed in pain, and was rushed to hospital.

Mohsin Ahmed, a fruit-seller at the scene, said: 'I was minding my own business when, out of the corner of my eye, I saw this man on the nearby bench hit himself on the stomach. He started shouting in pain, and fell down. I ran to him. He told me, "I was killing a mosquito."'

Ahmed and another passerby took Shettigar to hospital, but Shettigar was declared dead on arrival. This reporter personally examined his shirt, but it showed no signs of a dead mosquito. Shettigar had died in vain.

'Did you really examine his shirt?' Mohan asked me.

'Yes,' I replied.

'And there was no blood on it?'

'None at all.'

'Did he really tell the fruit-seller he was killing a mosquito?'

'Dude, what's the time?'

'It's 11.40.'

'Yes. We're already past the deadline. Do you want to do fact-checking now or finish the page and go for dinner?'

Mohan sighed. 'Dinner, dinner. Cool. And I like the last line, it's funny. I'm sure Boss will like it.'

'Boss can kiss my buttocks.'

'Boss is coming.'

I turned around. D'Souza was walking towards us.

'You're late again, Abir.'

'Sir, I work hard.'

'You need to work smart.'

'Sir, fuck you.'

Okay, I didn't say that last bit. D'Souza read my copy and was pleased. But it didn't make front page. Front page went to wardrobe malfunction.

I should introduce myself now. My name is Abir Ganguly. I work for a tabloid in Bombay called *The Afternoon Mail*. I am 23. I eat meat. I am heterosexual. I don't believe in God. I masturbate 11 times a day. I exaggerate frequently, as in the last sentence. I am ambitious, in the sense of what I want to *be* rather than what I want to *do*. There isn't particularly much I want to do, being very lazy, and I wish I could be rich and famous without having to do anything for it. That would be easy if I was rich and famous to start with. I'd make the Page 3 party pictures of *The Afternoon Mail* without any difficulty then, and would be like the restaurant owner Suhel Keswani, who is photographed every day at parties with hot women on each arm looking at him and going weak in the knees thinking: *Oh my God, he's sooo ugly and he smells sooo foul, but he's sooo rich, I'm wet already!*

But I'm not Suhel Keswani, I'm Abir Ganguly, and life being the way it is, I'll probably end up with his paunch and body odour and none of his money, which means there won't be any pretty women by my side but, at most, an old aunty from Byculla saying: *My son died of a heart attack. You reported he was trying to kill a mosquito. He died of a heart attack!*

Ya. But he's dead, no? So what difference does it make?

On my first day in this newspaper, a year ago, D'Souza came up to me and asked: 'So what kind of stories do you want to write for us, young man?'

'You tell me, sir.'

'No, you tell me. I want to see what you want to do first.'

'Sir, um, I want to do the kind of stories that reveal, um, what this city is all about.'

'What is this city all about?'

'Sir, um, this city, sir, has, um, lots of struggle, and life is hard, and...'

'Enough!'

'Um?'

'Enough. Do you watch movies?'

'Yes, sir.'

'Do you watch sports?'

'Yes, sir.'

'Why?'

'Er...'

'I'll tell you why. Because you want drama. Our lives are boring, so we want drama everywhere. That is why we gossip. That is why we peek into our neighbours' houses. That is is why we watch movies, watch sports. That is why readers buy *The Afternoon*

Mail. Drama! Now, I want you to understand one thing.'

'Yes, sir.'

'Your job, as a reporter, is to find drama. People want story: conflict, love, action, violence, sadness, regret. Give them story. You know those old clichés, "dog bites man" and "man bites dog"? I want "man bites dog". Every story you write must be "man bites dog". Drama!'

'Yes, sir.'

'Good. Now, if you're headed to the pantry, tell Shobhan to send me an adrak chai.'

I headed to the pantry.

◾

After filing the mosquito story, I waited for Mohan to finish so we could go for dinner together. He'd be done in about 45 minutes, and we would go to Dilli Durbar and order sensuously meltacious kababs and bitch about the world.

Or so I thought. I had no idea that in just a few minutes my life would change. Somewhere in Mahalaxmi, Inspector Vallabh Thombre was yawning, scratching his armpit, and thinking, *It's time to call Ganguly*.

The worst part about being a reporter is that you can't keep your mobile phone off. I'm on the crime beat, and have sources in the police, in morgues, in hospitals, and if there was an afterlife, I'd have sources in hell as well, calling me to say, *Is that Mr Ganguly? Sir, I'm calling from So-and-So bank, we would like to tell you about our balance transfer facility.*

See, that's the problem with not being able to turn off the phone. I wish all communication happened through carrier pigeons, so I could eat the ones sent by telemarketers.

Anyway, so Thombre called me. Cops have various reasons to call reporters, but the most common one is to tell them about a case they've cracked. Then their names appear in the newspapers and their wives read it and feel good about their marriage for about 30 seconds.

'Ganguly, Inspector Thombre. I hope I'm not disturbing.'

'Never, sirjee, that's not possible. Bolo, what's up?'

'Ganguly, I have story for you. I have received tip that few gangster from Chhota Sion gang are spending night in nearby housing society called Samruddhi. We are leaving to arrest. Why don't you come with photographer, you might get story, pictures.'

Chhota Sion is a mid-level don known for extorting money from builders. Was there an interesting angle to this somewhere? I wouldn't know until I got there. Maybe a lot of ransom money would be recovered from them. (*Ten Crore Recovered in Ten-Rupee Notes as Sion Gangster Breaks Down After Arrest.*) Maybe I could get to speak to one of them after the arrest. (*Sion Gangster Reveals Childhood Sexual Abuse by Priests.*) Maybe there would be a fierce gunfight in which all the cops and my photographer would be killed, and I would snatch Thombre's gun and shoot all the goons, heroically rescuing a six-year-old hostage girl whose nubile sister, rushing to the scene and whipping off her bra from under her shirt to staunch the flow of blood from my wounds in the absence of other bandage material, would be eternally (and carnally) grateful. (*Heroic Reporter Battles Goons, Becomes Sex Symbol of Mumbai.*)

Okay, maybe not that one.

'I'll be there, Thombresaab. Shall I come to the station?'

'Come fast, we will leave in half hour.'

■

Ten minutes later, I was on the back of Santosh Hegde's motorcycle. Santosh is one of our photographers, and often comes with me for late-night stories. It is his ambition to be a top fashion photographer one day. Well, actually, no – that is his fantasy, not his ambition. While he has the ability to do any kind of photography, it isn't just ability but personality that determines where we end up. He'll always be a tabloid photographer, shooting squalor while he dreams of glamour.

Santosh doesn't speak much on assignment. This is not because he is taciturn but, I believe, because he is bored. I can't blame him. All he does is shoot 'dog bites man'. Then my job kicks in.

We reached the station. Thombre was waiting for me outside, and gave me a broad smile. His hand rested on his paunch. His eyes were red. His hair was damp and neatly combed, as if preparing for a photoshoot. (At the most he'd get a quote. Photos of cops make no sense unless they're decapitated or suchlike.)

'Ganguly, Hegde, hello. I was waiting for you. Exciting story, gangster hideout, police investigation, bold arrest.'

Thombre often spoke in bullet points, and always in English, even though it was his third language. He would probably have been offended if we'd tried to chat with him in Marathi or Hindi, so we indulged him. His English skills were functional, and functional is all that matters in Bombay.

'Super,' I said. 'What's the back story? How did you know their whereabouts? What are you charging them under?'

'Tonight we will probably find drug, but we will file many charge: they are Chhota Sion gang, so there is extortion, attempted murder, theft. Cases have piled up like my backlogs in college. Ha ha. Come now, follow jeep.'

Thombre got into a jeep. A police van followed. Two cops on a motorcycle followed. We followed.

Twenty minutes later we drew up outside a housing society. The cops got down. One of them walked over to the watchman and said something. There was no one else around. The cops gathered near the entrance of one of the buildings as Thombre came to me and whispered: 'You two wait out. We will call when we are ready. You can take picture of arrest then. And don't worry if you hear gunshot.'

'What gunshot? There'll be firing?'

'No, we are not expecting. But it is gang. They have gun sometime. Don't worry – nothing will happen to us.'

His confidence unnerved me. I had expected a routine arrest, not one where there might be bullets fired and a bodycount. I hoped this would not turn out to be an encounter killing, with Thombre spinning a story of a gunfight, in which heroic cops risk their lives to take on hardened criminals. Was he using me to build his legend?

I'm a cynical bastard, I have to admit – but I'm an armchair cynic. I'm cynical about ideas and hopes and so on, abstract things that don't affect me directly. Being cynical about things that have consequences is harder.

I hoped there wouldn't be a gunfight. I hoped Thombre would quietly call us in after 10 minutes, and let Santosh take pictures of three handcuffed dudes and a table on which packets of cocaine had been spread out for display. Or even homeopathic powder. That would be just fine.

For a couple of minutes after the cops went in, nothing happened. Santosh lit a cigarette. We shuffled our feet. We listened to crickets. We looked at the watchman who avoided our gaze. We looked at windows. We waited for Thombre to call us.

Then we heard them: loud thuds in the distance, like big doors slamming shut, four or five of them. Then there was silence. We looked at each other. Santosh threw down his cigarette and stubbed it out with his shoe. I twirled my pen with my fingers, round and round and round.

For what seemed like half an hour but really was probably a few seconds, we heard no further sounds. Then we heard, in the distance, a woman's voice. She was shouting; then crying loudly. We heard a few male voices. Then we saw one of the constables emerge from the building. He saw us and stopped. Santosh shifted his camera from one hand to both. The constable hesitated, turned, went back inside.

We heard more noises: the woman's voice, and a couple of male ones — presumably the cops. There were no other sounds. No lights came on in any of the windows. No doors opened.

Then Thombre marched out with two of his men. He gestured to me to wait where I was. The three men discussed something. Then Thombre turned and walked towards me. As he did so, one of the cops with him said something like: *'Thank God he was Muslim.'*

I didn't hear it clearly then, but I remember it clearly now.

Thombre walked up to me and said: 'Listen, this was not what we expected.'

I blurted out: 'What, you shot the wrong guy?'

'No, no, no. We never shoot wrong guy. But there was not gang, there was one man. He try to shoot us. We shoot him. His name, Mohammad Iqbal.'

'He was a gangster?'

'Mohammad Iqbal. You can say, part of Chhota Sion gang. He open fire. We shoot him. Did you write that down? Mohammad Iqbal.'

'I got it.'

'I know there is not enough for proper news piece. I'm sorry for that. You do one of those brief report. No need to mention me.'

'Who was the woman?'

'Woman? Oh, some relative. It's okay. He was a gangster. We got him.'

'Okay.'

'You should leave now. In fact, you were never here. I will call.'

I didn't feel like going back home, so I asked Santosh to drop me at the office. All the editions had closed. I was the only person there. I might as well file this now, I thought. It would go into briefs: the collection of news snippets that comprised a headline and a few lines of text each. There would be no byline.

I switched on my computer. I started typing.

Headline: Cops Kill Gangster in Gunfight

Copy: A police team from Thane killed a local gangster, Mohammad Iqbal, at Samruddhi Housing Society in Mahalaxmi today. A group of policemen went to his house to arrest him at about 1.30am. Iqbal opened fire when they confronted him. The police fought back, and Iqbal was killed. None of the policemen were injured.

I copy-pasted the text into an email to the desk guys. Then, just before clicking 'send', I cut out the last line.

2. Meeting Muneeza

Despite all that had happened, I slept well. When I woke up, at two in the afternoon, my throat was dry. I needed to drink water, I needed to pee, I needed to go get some food. I could smell my socks. All my shirts were either dirty or unironed. I needed to open the window and let some fresh air in.

To be honest, the only thing that bothered me about the incident of the previous night was that I'd been there. I would otherwise have got the news from police briefings somewhere and reported it exactly as I eventually did. But I was there, and that made it messy. Thombre's story didn't feel right, but I could hardly have charged into the flat and carried out my own investigation – Thombre, on whose invitation I was there to begin with, wouldn't have allowed that.

What could have had happened? I thought it possible that Thombre's informer had got it wrong, and that they had knocked on the door of an innocent man. Maybe he'd opened the door half asleep, angry at being woken up, and had reacted belligerently without realizing what was going on. One of the cops, either trigger-happy or just nervous, fired. A woman emerged from behind the man. Then, by entering the house and seeing the trappings of family life, or by seeing a nameplate, or whatever, they realized that they'd made a mistake.

But this was conjecture.

I called up Thombre in the evening from the office. I asked him about Mohammad Iqbal. *Oh, he was criminal*, Thombre said casually. The gun that Iqbal had fired was evidence. They had also found drugs there. Open-and-shut case. Pity the man had to die, but that's how it was sometimes.

I had no reason to investigate further. I had no time either. *The Afternoon Mail* is demanding. Every day, across Bombay, men bite dogs. Reports are needed.

A week passed.

■

I was sitting at my desk quietly playing poker online, bothering no one, when the office peon walked over and said that Mahesh wanted to see me in his cabin. Mahesh is the chief editor of *The Afternoon Mail*. I trotted over.

When I got there, he was showing two women out of his office. One, middle-aged, wearing a beige sari, looked vaguely familiar, like either an old friend or a TV star. The other was a slim, teenage girl, maybe around 18 or 19, wearing an ill-fitting cheapish cotton salwar-kameez. There was clearly a class difference between the two women, and I wondered what they were doing there, and why Mahesh wanted to see me.

Mahesh shook hands with Beige Sari, nodded at the girl, and they went off. He turned his attention to me. 'Ah, Abir, I was looking for you. I hope you aren't busy. Come on in.'

Mahesh is in his mid-30s, and is the youngest newspaper editor in Bombay. He studied journalism abroad and was once a trainee at *The New York Times*. Then he returned to India, where we worship people with firang resumés, joined *The Times of India*, and then, oddly, ended up here three months ago. What can an ambitious journalist achieve at a tabloid?

I sat down. Mahesh said: 'Abir, how do you enjoy being on the crime beat?'

'It's good,' I replied. 'Sometimes it feels like a grind, but I prefer it to the other beats.'

'But do you feel satisfied? I've been seeing your work, and it's competent without being outstanding. I know you're capable of much more. You know that yourself. Is this the kind of work you want to do as the years go by?'

'Well, there isn't much scope for me to do much more than this here, is there?'

'*So far* there hasn't been. Abir, when I was about to leave my last job, I also had an offer to head the Sunday edition of a big national newspaper. That would have been more prestigious, and cushier. But I chose this. I chose this because I was passionate about local reporting, about getting inside the guts of a city and laying them out. There is no better place to do that than a newspaper like this, and no better city than Bombay to do it in. That is all people expect of a newspaper like ours: great local reportage. And I think we insult their intelligence by giving them sensationalist nonsense, and rubbish like that mosquito story you did last week.'

'Mahesh...'

'I'm not blaming you, it's a good story by the standards of this newspaper, but I'd like to give you a chance to go beyond that. Are you game?'

'I'd love to do something bigger in scope. But, er...'

'But what? I'll tell you. I have a story for you. See, we're starting a new section tentatively called "This is Your City". It will run every Saturday and will feature an in-depth report about one particular aspect of this city. We've laid down a number of areas we intend to look at in detail: how the municipality works, the nature of local politics and why people feel so disconnected from it, how crime and punishment mean different things to different classes of people. One of the specific areas I was thinking of for you is how law and order exist only for the rich and middle class, how the poor – which is most of this city – get screwed. And there's a particular story I have in mind that you could start working on right away.'

Yawn. Hmm?

'The lady who was just in here,' he continued, 'is Meenakshi Khanna, the social activist. You might have seen her on TV talk shows, she comes on a lot of those.'

That's why she had looked familiar.

'She runs an NGO called Teach Your Children,' said Mahesh. 'They do some good work educating children in the slums. But she was here regarding another matter. The girl who was with her, Muneeza, lives in Mahalaxmi, in a housing society called Samruddhi...'

Oh shit.

'...with her father. Or rather, she used to. Last week, some policemen came to her house at night. They shot her father in cold blood. It was clearly a mistake: the man has worked with Meenakshi for years now, he did the accounts in her office. Well, to justify the murder, the cops claimed that he was a gangster, and so on. I noticed that you filed a story about it the day after it happened. How did you get the news?'

'Er, Thombre called me and told me,' I blurted out. 'He's an inspector there, he's one of my regular sources.'

Ouch. Why had I lied? At that moment, sitting in front of Mahesh, I could hardly have said that I was there that night. A crime might have been committed, I suddenly realized. Was I an accomplice of some sort?

Thombre, I knew, would not reveal that I was there: it was in his interest to be low-key about this. And Santosh, well, his interests were the same as mine.

Mahesh was speaking. I hadn't been paying attention. I switched back on.

'...huge story in this somewhere. It's both investigative as well as human-interest. The investigative story is the obvious one, the police angle, and I've already commissioned a feature on such cases from the past. But it's the human-interest story that seems to me to have a lot of scope.

'So here's what I suggest,' he went on. 'You go and meet this girl Muneeza. Find out more about her father's life, and trace his journey over the years. There's a microcosm of India in there, and of Bombay. I suggest you do more than a 250-word report on this. In fact, I'll give you 3000 words if you want. Even 5000. Even more. Our new section will have that space, and we'll shake up local reporting with our stories. I just need to know one thing: Does the story excite you?'

What could I say? Every reporter dreams of doing stories like this, and Mahesh was offering me any word-count that I wanted. What kind of schmuck would turn it down?

'I'm game. But what's the deadline?'

'As long as it takes to get the story, Abir. This is a timeless story, and our new section won't be launched for at least two weeks. It may take even longer. We're not *The New Yorker*, and you can't take months over this. But I'll give you the space to do this story well. You'll work directly with me and show me the drafts. I've also asked D'Souza to relieve you of the crime beat for the time being till you finish this story.'

'Awesome,' I said. I had to feign the excitement I would no doubt have felt if I hadn't answered Thombre's call that night.

'Meenakshi's number is on this.' He handed me her card. 'I told her that one of my reporters would call her. She'll set up a meeting with Muneeza, and you could take it from there. Be sensitive, the girl just lost her father.'

◢

I went and spoke to Santosh. He agreed that it was not a good idea to tell people that we'd been there. If this became a scandal of some sort, our presence would put us in trouble.

It was clear, though, that Mahesh would not run a story about this murder, if that is what it was, right away. The cops would deny it, and the paper wouldn't have a good reason for not taking the police's word on the matter. It would seem like cheap sensationalism, and given that we were a tabloid, we could even be accused of fabricating details. That had happened in the past – and with good reason.

It was smarter, from Mahesh's point of view, to do a story on the dead man. If you could humanize him, and make the reader feel empathetic, then the story of his death would draw readers to their own conclusions. It was a great story to do, and if I wrote it well, I'd be noticed.

What about the conflict of interest? What conflict of interest? I wasn't there.

I can rationalize anything.

◾

Meenakshi called me over to her office at 10 in the morning the next day. It must have seemed a reasonable time to her. She probably woke up at six, did pooja, sent the kids to school, made her husband breakfast, showered, got dressed, reached her office and wrote the Mahabharata on a single grain of rice before 10. For me, 10 was closer to midnight than to morning. But I set an alarm for eight, hit 'snooze' nine times, and eventually managed to get up and rush to her office. I was only 15 minutes late.

'Hi, Abir,' she said as I entered her cabin. 'Sit down. Muneeza should be here any moment. Would you like some tea or coffee?'

'I wouldn't mind black coffee, if that's available.'

'Sure. Wait a minute.'

She went out of the room and presumably gave instructions to her minions. I looked around. Her room was untidy, fitting the NGO profile more than a corporate one, which shows that stereotypes are sometimes on the mark. There was a cane bookshelf loaded with old books, and a desk with files and an old IBM laptop from before it became Lenovo. A miniature porcelain cat sat on her desk, with its miniature tail unmoving, which meant it was happy to see me. There was a photo frame that faced her seat, so I couldn't see who was in it. (*Abir, that's a picture of me and Salman Khan, both of us bare-chested!*)

She came back in and sat down. 'Your coffee is coming. In the meantime, let me tell you something about Muneeza.

'Muneeza is not from a particularly well-off family, but she's well-educated. Her father had been working with me for the last 11 years, and her mother died in an accident when she was just nine. We made sure that

Muneeza joined a decent school and went to college. She's doing her graduation in commerce now. She's a very bright girl, and also very brave: I haven't seen her cry even once since this happened.'

'Hmm. How does she feel about this whole media business, this story being done on her father by me and so on?'

'Obviously she wasn't keen on it. At first she was outraged, and when she came to me, she wanted to fight the police. But she soon realized that not much would come of that. They'd set up an enquiry, no one would touch the cops, and Muneeza would end up in and out of courts for years and years. Plus she wouldn't be safe. She wasn't happy about it, but I gave her a reality check.

'And I admit,' Meenakshi continued, 'that I talked her into this. Mahesh is an old friend, I went to school with his elder sister, he's a first-class journalist. I just thought that there was a story here in the public interest. Of how, here is this good man who works hard all his life for good causes, and this is how he ends up.'

'I have one question. Did the Muslim bit hurt?'

'What Muslim bit?'

'I mean, that he's Muslim. Did that lend some credibility to the cops' case?'

'That's a good question. I would imagine it did. Look, if he was Hindu they could still say he was a naxalite or a Maoist insurgent or something, but that wouldn't be so credible, not in Bombay. But yes, he's Muslim, and that makes people who don't know him wary of presuming him innocent until proven otherwise. They could so easily appear antinational, you know what I mean. And these are such deplorably patriotic times.'

At this point the peon came in with a tray. The sugar was separate. I duly added, stirred, and as I took the first sip, Muneeza walked in. I stood up.

'Muneeza, meet Abir Ganguly from *The Afternoon Mail.*'

I extended my hand; she extended hers. She didn't have a grip, so effectively I held her hand for a moment and let it go. She looked at me once, keenly, and then looked away. For the rest of this meeting, she wouldn't look at me directly while speaking, but either down on the floor or past me. But when my eyes were pointed elsewhere, I could sense her looking hard at me, as if penetrating, with her gaze, all my thoughts. Our eyes hardly met.

'Hi, I'm so sorry about your dad,' I said softly. How does one say these things anyway? She nodded, and got to the point.

'What exactly is your newspaper planning to write?'

'Well, I was hoping that I could talk to you about your father, and do a sort of profile of him.

You know, how he was as a kid, how he grew up, where he worked, the kind of books he read, music he listened to, the things he believed in, and so on. Paint a picture of him so that readers feel like they've known him for—'

'What about his murder?'

'Yes, we'll come to that, but many people die in this city every day, and it's just a statistic for the reader unless I can flesh it out into—'

'My father was murdered. He was murdered in cold blood. What's the point of doing a profile of him as if he's a musician getting the Padma Shri or something? He was murdered! The murder is what you should write about. Your story should begin with the murder. It should be *about* the murder and those... those *bastards* who killed him.'

She used that word as if she'd never used it before, but needed it now to express her rage.

What could I say now? Her father *was* murdered in cold blood. That was the story. But that was not the story I was here to write.

'Muneeza, don't misunderstand me. But here's what it is: if I write about a man named Mohammad Iqbal getting murdered by a bunch of cops who claim he was a gangster, it's a story no one cares about as long as Mohammad Iqbal is just a name. But if I can write about the man, make people feel that they know this man, make them start caring, then the murder matters to them, then they feel outraged.'

'Why are you doing this?'

'Doing what?'

'Doing this story? Asking questions about my father? Why? Do *you* care about him?'

Now our eyes met. I had no answer to this question, and she knew that, and I knew she knew that, and so on. I would not be able to explain to her that our interests were aligned here, even if we wanted different things, for that would be no match for the logic of her emotion. *Did I care?* Not for Mohammad Iqbal, and not for his daughter Muneeza. I was using them, and I couldn't tell a girl who had just lost her father: *Use me too.*

Meenakshi intervened. 'Muneeza, we've spoken about this—'

'I know we did,' said Muneeza. 'But I don't see the point anymore. My father's gone, and now you want me to sit and talk about him, and what a good person he was, and what a good father he was. What's the point? He's gone!'

No one spoke for a few seconds. We didn't look at one another. My coffee was cold. I put the cup down.

'I'm sorry,' she said. 'I'm getting too emotional. This is not like me. I'm sorry, can we talk some other time? I'm very tired. I haven't been sleeping.'

Meenakshi and I looked at one another. I got up.

'Listen, Muneeza, I'm sorry,' I said. 'I'm truly sorry you've lost your father. I lost my father too, once, though it wasn't so sudden and it wasn't such a shock. I don't like to talk about it either. Let me call you some other time, and if you don't want to do this, then I won't ask you again. I wish I could help...'

'Thanks, no, I'm just tired...'

'Do you have a number I could call?'

She looked at Meenakshi, then at me, and gave me her telephone number. 'This is my aunt's home,' she said. 'I'm staying with her for now. Call me tomorrow morning, before eight. I might leave for college then.'

'Okay,' I said. 'Bye.'

I said goodbye to Meenakshi as well, told her it had been nice meeting her, and walked out. I didn't feel like going to office. I didn't feel like going home either. So for an hour I walked around, and then, too tired to walk anymore, I sat down at a Marine Drive katta and watched the sad excuse that some of us call the sea.

3. Dreams, Malls and Sancho Panza

I hate setting alarms: it means that I have to get up earlier than I normally would, and that is surely against the natural order of things. The pleasures of life are to be had in bed, awakening, finding no urgent need to get up, closing one's eyes, caressing the pillow by one's side (entirely non-sexually) and drifting away again. But here I was, for the second day in a row, setting an alarm for an obscene hour. I'd probably hit snooze a couple of times, then get up and call Muneeza, and hopefully she would... what? I didn't even know what I was hoping for.

Did I want to do this story? I did. At first I had no option, my editor had told me to do it, but then I sold it to myself, turning contingency into choice. I wanted to write about Mohammad Iqbal. I wanted to write the kind of story that would make journalists and readers everywhere notice my name. I wanted the big magazines to call and say, 'Do something for us. Anything. You can have all the space you want.'

Fuck, I was fantasizing again. I turned off the light. I closed my eyes. I dreamt.

In my dream, I woke up and it was 10. I shot up, grabbed the phone and called Muneeza.

Thombre answered.

'I was waiting for your call, Ganguly. You are late. We got here before you. We receive tipoff that Muneeza Iqbal was gangster. When we got here, she open fire. We fought back heroically, she is dead now. Hegde is here, he is taking photograph. He want to be fashion photographer.

'But I have question for you, Ganguly: Why the fuck was she waiting for your call?'

I woke up and went to pee. Normally I don't get up to pee in the middle of the night. Sometimes the urge comes, but my laziness beats my need-to-pee-ness and I hang in there till morning. But this time I felt restless, so I did what I had to.

In another dream I heard my doorbell ring. I

went and opened the door. There was no one there. I went back to sleep.

◾

'Ganguly, what is an adjective?' my teacher asked.

'Good,' I replied.

'Good?'

'Good is an adjective,' I said. Mrs Shastri glared at me. The class burst out laughing. But they were mocking me, not appreciating my subtle if unintended wit.

◾

What kind of fucking stupid dreams are these? When will the alarm ring?

◾

Everytime I woke up that night, I felt wide awake. Then morning came, the alarm rang, and I was sleepy, so sleepy, hitting snooze with such entreatment, hoping five minutes would last for ten or twenty. I stumbled out of bed at 7.50, drank a glass of water, and called Muneeza.

'I can meet you today,' she said. 'I'm not going to college.'

'Great,' I said. 'What time suits you, and where should we meet? You want me to come to your place?'

'No, no. Can I meet you somewhere outside? Where is your office, why don't we meet somewhere there? I can come there.'

'Um, I actually won't be going to office till evening. What time were you planning to meet?'

'Would 9.30 be okay?'

Damn. Nine-thirty would mean that I'd have to get ready in a hurry, and I hated that.

'Listen, why don't we have lunch somewhere, if that's okay with you. You want to come to Eterniti Mall? There's a food court there that has lots of options, and since today is a weekday, it won't be too crowded.'

She hesitated, and then said, 'Okay. I'll be there. What time exactly?'

'What about one?' I said. 'We can do lunch and then sit and talk over coffee.'

'Okay,' she said.

'See you there.'

It's fashionable to diss malls these days. One of the opinion columnists at *The Afternoon Mail*,

TV Iyengar, keeps ranting about malls and *rampant consumerism* and *predatory globalization* in his columns. The other day, I saw him in Eterniti, wife and one kid in tow, all of them munching on falafel sandwiches. They had what appeared to me to be 121 packets of shopping beside them. They looked happy.

◾

I like Eterniti Mall because of the giant bookstore in it, Bookends. I can spend hours there, and my idea of a perfect afternoon on my days off is to go there and pick up some books and magazines and sit down and have a sandwich and a couple of cups of coffee.

I saw this disgusting TV commercial recently in which a boy gives his elder sister a surprise gift. What is it, she asks, as she begins to unpack it. A book, says the boy. The girl looks disappointed, until she unwraps her gift and finds that it is a box of chocolates. Then the bimbette cheers up.

My world is the other way around: a book is the best possible gift you can give. I enjoy being among books – especially in air-conditioning.

Having said that, all the girls I've ever gifted a book to looked like they'd have preferred chocolates.

◾

Muneeza was a few minutes late. She was wearing a well-fitting blue kurta with a white churidar, a contrast to the loose and somewhat shabby salwar-kameez she had worn the last two days. Her hair was tied back in a ponytail, and she held two big plastic bags in her hand. She gave me a half-smile, perhaps unable to decide if a full smile was appropriate, or whether she knew me well enough to grace me thus, or maybe because I was simply an opportunistic prick in her eyes.

After the hi-hellos I asked her what she wanted to eat.

'I don't know, what's good here?'

'You've never been here before?'

'Er, no, not here. What were you planning to eat?'

'I'm not too hungry, so I was going to grab myself a sandwich at Subway. Would you like one as well?'

'Yes, I think I'll try.'

We walked over to the Subway counter, and I realized that this was her first time at a Subway: she walked into the veg half of the counter and asked if they had a chicken sandwich. I realized that I had to be sensitive about more than just her father's death here – and I had to make sure I paid.

She stumbled through her order, and when I drew out my wallet she said: 'I'll pay for myself, thanks.'

'No, please, my office pays for this,' I lied. 'This goes on my expense account.'

I could imagine my colleagues at work convulsing in laughter if they ever heard what I'd just said. My father used to say: *It doesn't matter what you do in life, as long as you do it well.* No one lies with as much panache as I do.

■

I guided Muneeza towards a corner table. We sat and ate in silence. I didn't know what small talk to make, and besides, my mother once said: *Never eat with your mouth full. I mean speak. Never speak with your mouth full.*

I finished before Muneeza and asked her if she wanted coffee or gelato or something, and she said she was fine, thank you. I went and got coffee for myself. As I returned, I saw that she had finished her food and was nervously fingering the plastic bag in her lap. I sat down.

'You wanted to know about my father,' she said. 'I've brought some photo albums so you can see some pictures of him.'

'That's great, thanks,' I said, though it hadn't struck me that I might want to see his pictures. But now that she'd got these albums, I realized the silliness of trying to paint a picture of this man for readers when I did not even know what he looked like. She handed me one of the albums, a large one with a tattered plastic cover with flowers on it.

'This is their wedding album,' Muneeza said. 'They got married in 1987. Wait, I'll tell you who's who.' She shifted from across me to sit on the side of the table, so she could point out the characters in her story.

The first picture was of a young man and woman getting married. He was dressed in a beige sherwani and shalwar, and a boat-shaped cap. He looked young: the growth of hair on his face was that of an adolescent, of the age when boys begin to think of themselves as men but no one else does.

'How old was he?' I asked.

'Oh, he wasn't as young as he looks in the pictures,' Muneeza said. 'He was 21. My mother was 19. They had an arranged marriage.'

'What was her name?'

'Rehana,' she said.

Rehana Iqbal was a tall woman, almost as tall as her husband. In these pictures she was slim and fair and demure, a matrimonial ad come to life. Her head was covered, and though she wore a fair amount of make-up, she didn't look ghastly with it, as so many Indian women do at their weddings. She was much better looking than her husband, as is common for Indian couples.

I turned the pages. Muneeza introduced me to a couple of uncles and aunts, but then stopped. I flipped through the pages, unsure of how long I should look at the photographs, and whether turning the pages too fast would be rude. We finished the album, I muttered 'nice' or something equally banal, and she passed me another, smaller album.

This showed the family through the ages. The first picture had the Iqbals posing awkwardly at a photo studio – but as I turned the pages, they relaxed more and more, as if they were getting more comfortable in their skins. Muneeza turned up on the third page, wailing as her parents held her. On the fourth page, she was placid, and a little bigger. On the fifth, she was on the floor with a cat, puzzled by it, smiling at it.

'That's a really sweet picture,' I said, for it was. Muneeza kept her eyes down.

As I turned the pages, her mother disappeared. I did not ask – there would be time for that later – and she did not say anything about it.

I flipped through the other albums a little quicker. Her father grew up quickly: he put on weight, his face lost its smoothness, and from the callow youngster he looked like in his wedding pictures, he changed into a man bearing all the burdens of the world. He grew a beard, and his early look of youthful sincerity changed to one of sombre reflection. (Or just boredom?) I wondered if he would have looked different if his wife had lived: more cheerful, perhaps, or clean-shaven, or just lighter? In the later pictures, he looked as if he bore all the gravity of the world, even when he smiled, even when he had his arm around the young Muneeza, awkwardly, as if he was still not at ease with the body language of paternal intimacy.

Muneeza was a beautiful child. She smiled in all her pictures, not like most people do – *cheese!* – but in a friendly, uninhibited manner, as if to tell the camera: *When you're done with your work I'll take you to my room and show you my toys and then we'll play.* It wasn't that she was plain now – but she looked tired and worn out, and her smiles were either polite, or they held something back.

I glanced at her quickly as I turned another page. If I'd met her in different circumstances, if she was well-dressed and cheerful, I would have found her attractive. She had a slender, well-proportioned face with a pretty smile, and her petite frame, even now, was poised and elegant. She carried herself well, and if I had seen her holding a cocktail glass at a party, I would have been tempted to flirt with her. (Of course, I wouldn't *actually* have flirted, because I'm such a coward, I am.)

I finished looking through the albums, and she put them away, one by one, carefully, into her plastic bag. Then she looked at me with a question mark on her face.

'Shall we talk about your dad a bit now?' I asked.

'Yes, okay.'

I took out my notebook from my pocket. 'I'll take some notes if you don't mind,' I said. She nodded.

I had some questions ready, but I assumed I wouldn't need to look at them once we got rolling. I didn't intend to write down every detail she gave me. I'd listen more than write, get a sense of what she was saying, and go back to her for any details I needed while writing the story.

'What is your earliest memory of your father?' I asked.

'Earliest?'

'Or rather, any early memory you have from your childhood, something he did or said or told you, which you remember strongly for some reason.'

I hoped I wasn't asking the wrong questions. I had clear memories of my father, little pictures that, put together, would perhaps tell a person a lot about him: how he would go out on Sundays to buy us ham and salami and then we'd have sandwiches in the evening; how he'd buy comics for me in bulk, and hide them, and give me a few at a time whenever I was bored or upset; how he'd swear loudly when he got angry, much to my mother's annoyance, and tell me later: *Abir, you should never use bad words or raise your voice in anger. I know I do it. But it is wrong, and I am not perfect. I want you to be better than me.*

But would I tell a stranger these things? Was it not safer to ask for some mundane biographical details and start from there?

'It's silly, I don't know if it helps, but the strongest memory I have of him from childhood is when I was a young girl and my mother died. Before that time, I used to be scared of him. He was this remote person who was rarely at home. I don't think I spent much time with him. And then, when my mother died, he broke down and cried like a baby when they came to take her before the funeral. They came to take her body, and he refused to let them. He stood by the bed and wept and did not allow anyone to touch her. But then he gave way, and became strong again. I looked at him differently after that. I saw that he wasn't strong at all, he was only acting. I also saw that someone loved my mother as much as I did — which surprised me.

'Until that day,' she continued, 'I'd loved him because he was my father, and he was around, and you love fathers. But I began to understand him much better when that happened. And we grew closer after that. He became a very loving father — he rarely showed his affection outwardly, he wasn't too demonstrative — but he always showed me that he cared for me, in his own way. And while he had a temper, he never, even once, shouted at me after my mother died.'

I hadn't written down a word yet. I suspected I wouldn't need to. How vulgar it would be to now scribble something like *'Wife's death, cried, grew more affectionate towards daughter'*.

'What was he like otherwise? How did he like spending his free time? Did he read, listen to music, did he take you to watch movies...?'

'He read a lot – a habit I picked up from him. When I was younger, he read on Islam and the Quran and so on, but as we grew older, he started reading more of other things. He read novels – he told me that he was unfortunate not to read enough when he was younger, but would start now. He joined a library, and we often sat and read together in the evenings. For example, one time he brought *Don Quixote* and *Wuthering Heights* home together, and he read one while I read the other. Then we exchanged. Then we discussed the books. I told him I want to be like Don Quixote. He told me, no, he read the book first, he's the Don Quixote of the house! So I said okay, then I'll be Sancho Panza!

'From that day on, he called me Sancho. That was my nickname from then!'

She was smiling, she looked so happy as she remembered this, and I smiled too. 'I don't want to hurt your feelings,' I said, 'but you don't look like a Sancho Panza to me. You look like a Muneeza.'

'Well, then you can't see well enough. I'm Muneeza *and* I'm Sancho.'

She looked down at the table and blinked a couple of times, perhaps thinking that such levity wasn't appropriate so soon after her father died. She raised her arm to push her hair back behind her ears, and left her elbow resting on the table, like a chess player deep in thought. Then she looked at her watch.

'Listen, I'm sorry,' she said. 'I need to go, it's three. I told my aunt I'll be at her place by four, and it'll take me an hour to get there. I'd meant to tell her I'll leave here at four, but I got confused.'

'No problem,' I said. 'Can we meet again?'

'Yes, sometime tomorrow?'

'Cool. Shall we meet here?'

'Yes, that sounds fine. What time? Morning 10 o'clock?'

'Okay. 10 o'clock.'

Damn. Why did I say 10 o'clock? Alarm, snooze, snooze, snooze...

◣

I went to the office and saw Mahesh. 'I've been working on the story,' I told him. 'I met Muneeza at Meenakshi's office yesterday, and I just met her today, and I'm spending some time with her tomorrow as well.'

'How's it coming along?'

'Well, it's going to be slow, Mahesh. We spent two hours together speaking about her father, and I feel like I've only just begun to get to know him.'

'No problem, Abir. I don't want you to hurry too much and give me a crap story. I want a great story. By when can I see a first draft?'

'Er, one week from now? Next Friday? Is that okay?'

Mahesh paused, probably for effect, and then said reluctantly: 'Okay, I'll expect your draft by Friday morning. You have a week. But it better be good. This is a big deal, my giving you so much time, D'Souza is upset with me. I've taken a gamble here. Get me the jackpot!'

'Er, yes, I'll try my best. Thanks a lot!'

Mahesh was right, this was outrageous. I'd been on the story two days, and he'd just given me another week just to see a draft. This was unheard of in our newspaper, and I knew I had to deliver something special. I was getting this one chance to lift my game, and if I didn't grab it, I'd be calling cops and morgue registrars for the next few years, enquiring about deaths, hoping someone had died in an interesting way, hoping I could spin it and get a headline out of it. I was tired of that, though I hadn't realized it until now. I needed to move on.

4. Commerce is Very Boring

That evening my friend Rahul came online to chat.

Rahul: abirda!

Abir: Hey, what's up?

Rahul: how's things?

Abir: Good, good. You?

Rahul: perfect... hey, dude, who was the chica I saw with u today?

Abir: What chica? With me?

Rahul: yo... at eternity... cosy u 2 looked, i thought i should not be kabab mein haddi

Abir: Haddi my ass. Dude, that was work. A girl I was meeting for a story. I'm doing a story on her father.

Rahul: ya ya, "we're just friends", lol... she looked cute... so u're not dating her?

Abir: No, no, of course not.

Rahul: cool, next time i see u then i'll come, u intro me.

Abir: I'll intro my ass.

Rahul: hey, abirda, u're my friend, dude, yo the man... she your rakhi sister or something?

Abir: Listen, I have to go. The boss is calling. You take care, man.

Rahul: good night and shabba khair, lol!;)

Waking up the next morning was not as hard as the previous two. In fact, I got up on my own five minutes before the alarm, didn't hit snooze, and didn't feel as grouchy as I usually did. I thought about the story. How would I structure it?

I needed to start with an anecdote, something personal and telling about Mohammad Iqbal. Muneeza had given me some interesting material the previous day. I took my notebook and started writing:

When Rehana Iqbal died, Mohammad Iqbal, her husband, stood beside her body and refused to let go. He cried like a baby. His daughter, Muneeza, just nine then, stopped crying as she sat on the bed and looked at him curiously. This was, she told me, the first time she had seen him like this. In time, she would get to know this side of him, perhaps the only real side of him, and love him with the same fierce intensity that he had shown that day by his dead wife's bed.

When they came to take Mohammad Iqbal's body away, though, she let him go. She was 18. He was shot dead, in cold blood, by a group of policemen...

No, I thought, not happening. Too maudlin, *the only real side of him.* Too clichéd, *fierce intensity.* Too faux dramatic, *in cold blood,* etc. This was hackwork. I needed to do better.

One more try:

> Mohammad Iqbal fought with his daughter to be Don Quixote, and she let him win. Iqbal, a...

No, I didn't yet know enough about him. I needed, to begin with, to get more meat, more biography. Since he had worked with Meenakshi, meeting her would be helpful. And I needed to ask Muneeza more personal questions about her dad. From Meenakshi, get an idea of the public Mohammad Iqbal; from Muneeza, the private man. I had been worried about being too intrusive – but yesterday Muneeza hadn't made me feel that way: she'd been forthcoming, quite willing to share personal details about her father.

She seemed to be getting over his death well enough. Or maybe not – maybe she was just pulling along, putting on a brave face. Just smiling so close to his death must feel like such a betrayal. I needed to find out more about her private life, I decided: who else she considered family, what they were like, what her friends were like, where she looked to for support.

Of course, this story wasn't about her.

I reached Eterniti and hung around in Bookends, as I'd told her I would. At about 10.15 she arrived, breathless.

'Sorry I'm late, my bus got stuck in a jam.'

'That's cool, no problem, I can wait forever in a bookshop. Do you want to go outside or do you want to browse?'

'Anything.'

'Let's go and have some coffee, we can come back here later.'

We walked out. She was wearing a shapeless pink knee-length kurta and a loose white salwar with hideous embroidery on the wide poncha at the bottom. If Rahul saw her with me today, he wouldn't want an intro — he'd probably think she was the kind of girl who travelled on buses.

I got myself a coffee and sold her into having an iced tea, which I picked up with my expense account. Then we sat down.

'How much more do you need to ask?' she said.

'Er, quite a lot actually. Sorry, is this taking up too much of your time?'

'No, not that way. It's just that, I was thinking about it, and I haven't understood what you're going to write about my father. He's done nothing special in life, so what can you say?'

'Well, Muneeza, this is not really a celebrity profile. It's more of a story, really. You read novels and short stories, don't you? They have stories about ordinary people, but they make us care about them. That's what I'm trying to do with my story.'

'And what is the point of that? Will they open a case for my father? Will they punish the policemen?'

'Well, it'll at least expose the rot in the system.' I was speaking in clichés; I hated that. 'And who knows, it might provoke enough outrage for something to happen.'

'A newspaper story?'

'Er...'

'A newspaper story can't change the world. I live in the real world. I know the real world. No one cares about newspapers. It only matters who holds the danda.'

I was worried that this conversation was going the way of our first one, at Meenakshi's office. Then she stopped.

'I'm sorry, Abir, it's not your fault, I should not get upset at you. But it's very difficult.'

This was the first time she'd said my name. Then she frowned and started to cry. She put her elbows on the table and, after a gesture of apology, looked down and held her head in her hands. A couple passing by looked at me disapprovingly, as if I was a cruel lover who had just refused to marry his pregnant girlfriend.

I had no idea how to deal with this. My first instinct, which lasted just a moment, was to put my arms around her and hold her. My next was to touch her arm and say something stupid like *there, there.* But I didn't know her well enough to touch her, so I just sipped my coffee awkwardly. After a few seconds, she wiped her eyes. I must seem so cold to her, I thought, sitting there unaffected. But what could I say?

She excused herself to go to the loo. 'Sure,' I said.

Perhaps I should have shown her to the loo. She didn't know where it was, and went around the food court clockwise, then counter-clockwise, and just as I was about to get up and guide her, she saw the sign and walked towards the corridor it pointed at. Just before she went in, she turned to look at me, saw that I was following her progress, and gave me an embarrassed smile.

It was the sweetest smile I'd ever seen. *I'd better not feel attracted to her*, I thought. *Look at how she's dressed!*

She returned, and came and stood by my side and ruffled my hair and said that she didn't intend it to be this way, but she had fallen in love with me. 'I hope they don't kill you as well,' she said.

Okay, this didn't happen. She returned.

As she sat down, I made a weak joke to the effect of her iced tea getting cold, and she half-smiled politely. I didn't want to go straight to the subject of her father, so I decided to make some small talk. The first thing that came to mind was cricket. But she wouldn't be following bloody cricket.

'So where do you study?' I asked.

'I'm studying commerce at JG College.'

'Do you like commerce?'

She shrugged. 'I wanted to study arts, do English literature. But Abbu felt that I needed to do something that would get me a job, so I could look after myself.'

Damn. We were talking about her father again. Even though my purpose of meeting her was to talk about her father, there was nothing I wanted to do less at this time.

'What about you? How long have you been a journalist?'

'Two years.'

'Did you do a course in journalism?'

'No, courses are useless. I just did the round of newspapers, wrote sample stories, got a job at almost no salary, and then became a cog in the machine.'

'Do you like what you do?'

'Well, I always thought it would be more glamorous than it is. I guess many jobs that look like fun from the outside are just drudge work when you get down to it.'

'Your family is also in Bombay?'

'No, I live alone. I've rented a one-bedroom flat in Andheri. My mother lives in Calcutta.'

'Do you like Bombay?'

'I like Bombay. Sure. Commuting is a pain, but the city's full of life, and I feel comfortable here, even though I'm from outside. You?'

'I've grown up in Bombay,' she said, 'and I love it and hate it also. I want to go out of here.'

'Where do you want to go?'

'Anywhere. I can't take it anymore in this city. I want to leave.'

'Yes, life can get a bit fast...'

'It's not that. It's not fast that's the problem.'

'Then?' I thought she'd bring her dad up; because he died here, and he was treated like shit, she wanted to leave.

'I just want a different life where I'm a totally new person, and I can start again.'

I was about to say *Commerce is very boring*, but it made no sense. 'I know what that's like,' I said. 'Even I'd like to go away somewhere.'

I got another cup of coffee and we chatted for a while, more like friends than like a journalist and a source of information. We didn't talk about her father, but I did get to know more about her life. Her only other family was an aunt who lived in Borivali, and that's who she was staying with now. Since her father's death, she hadn't gone home. She couldn't bear the thought of being in that house alone, so she only went there with her aunt or with a college friend called Sonal. The flat's lease would run out in a few weeks. She obviously could not afford to renew it. Nor did she want to stay with her aunt, whom she hated. She thought maybe she'd look for a girls hostel somewhere. Her father had some money in his bank account and she was the nominee. She thought she could manage with that till college got over, and then she could find a job. In an emergency, her aunt would help, because she was family – but Muneeza would never ask. She would manage.

I was surprised at how openly she was telling me these things. The previous day I'd assumed it was because of the story I was writing on her father, but now it no longer seemed that way – most of these details had nothing to do with that story. Maybe she just needed someone to speak to when I popped up. She didn't seem to have an active social life, and Sonal was the only friend she mentioned, the only friend at her father's funeral. This scared me a little. I couldn't afford to be too casual about this. I couldn't just do the story and walk away.

I suppose it was a burden. Strangely, I didn't mind it.

It was time for her to go. 'But we didn't speak about my father at all!'

'That's okay. If it's fine with you, we can do that some other time. I enjoyed spending time with you. When would you like to meet again?'

'Um, I can meet tomorrow.'

'That sounds good. Same place?'

'Okay.'

'Listen, if you come with enough time on hand, we can catch a movie also. My friends say *Lives of Others* is very good.'

She didn't say anything, just kept walking.

I felt awful when I saw her crossing the road to get to the bus stand when we were outside.

My phone rang at 8.30 that night.

'Hi, is that Abir?'

'Speaking.'

'This is Muneeza.'

'Oh! Hi, Muneeza.'

'I just called to say, I can't make it tomorrow morning, some work has come up.'

'Oh. What work?'

'Some work.'

'Ah, well, okay. When can we meet then? Day after?'

'I don't know.'

'Er, I have to get this story done by next Friday...'

'So we could have spoken about my father today, no?'

'Well, yes...'

'And also, I don't think I can come and see a film with you. That's not why we're meeting.'

'Oh, okay...'

Then silence.

'Okay then, bye, Abir.'

'Wait, Muneeza, one sec... How do I find out when you're free to meet next? Should I call you at your aunt's on Monday?'

'Um, no, you don't need to do that. Can we meet day after, same time?'

'Sure, see you on Monday then, same time, Eterniti.'

'Bye.'

She hung up. I was sure she had no other work tomorrow. She would spend the morning moping instead of being with me. And, despite being with me, I would also mope. We had that in common.

5. Sunday Bloody Sunday

Sunday came, and I woke up late and headed over to office. I didn't have to go, but I didn't have broadband at home, and I wanted to surf the net for a while. I figured I'd order lunch at work and then go hang out at the Bookends branch near office. Maybe I'd catch a film. I didn't feel like meeting any friends today.

D'Souza was skulking around as I made my way to my desk. 'Ah, the star feature writer is back at work. Good to see you, Ganguly. How's the story going? We expect a Pulitzer from this.'

Annoyed by his sarcasm, I leapt up and kicked D'Souza in the face, and he landed on his back, broke his spine, and never walked or kissed again.

Okay, I didn't.

'I'm okay, sir. Nice haircut. You look like Aamir Khan.'

D'Souza turned to see himself in the reflection of a whiteboard on his right. Yea! But he quickly turned back.

'But how's the story going, I asked.'

'Very good, sir, I'm still collecting all my material. It's nice of you to relieve me from my regular duties.'

'Hmm. Good, good, I hope it turns out well. Let me know when you're ready to be back on the beat, I put that new trainee, Kolhatkar, on the job, and he's almost as slow as you were when you began.'

'Ya, sure.'

'Grmph.'

D'Souza walked off and I sighed and switched on my computer. It took a week to boot, because of which I missed my deadline.

◾

My surfing routine is boringly predictable. I go to Rediff, whose headlines are often a hoot – I especially take an adolescent delight in 'Top MFs'. That's 'Top Mutual Funds', but I always read it as 'Top Motherfuckers', and dream of starting a similar feature at *The Afternoon Mail*. Rediff is also where I first read my all-time favourite headline: 'Eight Baby Crocodiles Die of Stress.' That sums up our times so well.

Then I go to India Uncut, the only blog I read every day. I like its WTF section – my reaction to life around me is more and more summed up by those three letters. I suppose it's condescending of me to react like that, and when I'm no longer so young, I might find myself part of the WTFness, no longer able to laugh. We shall see.

I spend about half an hour at the start of my day checking my email – and probably a couple more, as the day goes on, in Easy Surfing Instalments. Would any of the 877 people who write to me regularly bother to do so if they had to use pen and paper, and then physically post the thing afterwards? I doubt it. I also doubt that more than one-hundredth of my Facebook friends are true friends in real life as well – but it's all good. I'm connected; I'm empowered; I love the internet. Also, there's porn.

Much of the time I spend surfing the web goes on porn. I'm lucky that I sit with my back to a wall in office, and no one can see my computer. I'm sure our IT guys spy on me, though – with great pleasure.

When I was growing up, in the pre-internet days, porn was just naked chicks, nothing more to it. But now it's like Starbucks – just as we're bewildered by 8014 kinds of coffee, we are faced with 64,319 categories of porn. There's Black Hair Sex. There's Goth Sex. There's High Heels and Indian Sex. There's Messy, Pantyhose, Panties, Tit Fucking, Bikini Babe Sex, Spanking and Machine Fucking. I feel conventional clicking on Voyeurism and Amateur Sex, as I tend to do.

If sociologists a hundred years later look at the screenshot of a standard porn aggregator, with all its categories, they'll get a hell of a snapshot of our times. Even stressed-out baby crocodiles can't compete – unless there's a category for them too. (*BabyCrocs in Leather?*)

Lazily clicking through the sites I visit, I landed up at desi-khatiya.com, with its famous alliterative galleries. The latest ones were of Antsy Anjali, Randy Ramola, Pretty Preeti, Desperate Dimple and Mmmm Muneeza. Mmmm Muneeza? I clicked.

This Muneeza was a big-boned woman with artificially large breasts and the most unattractive pout ever. I mentally replaced her face with that of my Muneeza.

Nausea came. I shut down the browser. I played Hearts. I played Hearts badly, and kept getting the queen of spades and most of the hearts without shooting the moon. I felt angry with myself.

I ordered lunch with three of my colleagues. We sat and ate in the common area of the office. They argued about Sachin Tendulkar, and whether he was past it, and should retire. I would normally be quite vociferous on this subject. Today, I found it pointless. What would our talking about it achieve?

Did Tendulkar have a webcam and microphone installed where we were sitting? Would it make any difference to him? Would he carry it in his mind the next time he went to bat, thinking, *Today I must make a century, and as that wise subeditor in that noted tabloid said, I should refrain from playing outside the off stump when the ball is new*?

Besides, nothing that these guys were saying was new, especially to them. It was like their minds were in a loop – hit a subject, and the same mediocre thoughts would pop up, and they'd go through the motions of 'thinking' like they went through the motions of existing. How pointless. And I was just like them, on most days. My whole life was this.

I was now overcome by self-loathing. This was not a good thing, because if I stopped thinking highly of myself, who would? I figured I'd go to Bookends now, read a good book, have lots of coffee, check out some pretty chicas, and not think about that blasted piece I had to do.

◢

Having said that, lunch wasn't all that bad. Good keema-kaleji is better than sex, I reminded myself. I can have it by myself, and it's never awkward.

◢

I didn't go to Bookends after all. Seema, a trainee, suggested that we should go watch a movie. Five of us went forth. I cracked ironic jokes about the world and our colleagues. They thought I was in a good mood. We didn't get tickets for the show. (It was a Sunday. Which fool expects to go to the hall and get tickets on a Sunday?) One of the guys suggested that we hang out at TGIF. I didn't feel like it. It would be crowded and noisy, and they'd blast the music so loudly that we wouldn't be able to hear each other, and we'd be SCREAMING INANE SMALL TALK ACROSS THE TABLE. I excused myself and left.

I hate Sundays. Everywhere you go it's crowded. You take a walk on Marine Drive, and half the 82 billion of Bombay have landed up there, and everyone's jostling you. How can you take a stroll in an adventure course? You go to any of the malls – especially Eterniti – and they're full of crass husbands and self-conscious wives and misbehaving children and teenagers from hell. Even Bookends is packed. You stand between two shelves looking at the one in front of you and a rotund gentleman with body odour pretends he's making his way past you. You shift forward to let him pass, but he doesn't – he just occupies the space you vacated. Now you're copulating with the shelf in front, where you can no longer see anything, and you're butt-to-butt with the fat guy. So you have to move. You go out and the streets are teeming. You feel hungry but the cafés are full. You contemplate an early dinner, but no matter how early you make it to the restaurant of your choice, they tell you you'll have to wait an hour-and-a-half. *'Come back in 2010,'* I expect someone to say to me any day.

And then you go home, and even there they won't leave you alone. There's Vallabh Thombre standing by the door, holding a gun, scratching his crotch, feeling up his paunch, chewing gutkha, spitting it at your wall. There's Santosh Hegde at his feet, taking pictures of him, saying, *One more shot, just one more shot.* There's D'Souza sitting in my chair at the computer table. There's Mohan polishing his shoes. There's a portrait of Mahesh on the wall from which he chucks cigarette stubs onto my floor. There's Seema on the divan with four sweaty subeditors flirting ineptly with her as they play with themselves. And in my bedroom, where I go to escape, there's Muneeza sitting on my bed, and she's looking very beautiful, and she's wearing something nice, but she looks unhappy. And on the bed, by her side, there is something, someone, covered from head to toe in my blanket.

I went home, napped, woke up, showered, and sat down in front of my computer to make a list of all the things I needed to find out about Mohammad Iqbal. So far, I knew little about the father and more about the daughter. I had been very unsystematic about this. I needed to go to my next meeting better prepared.

Things to ask about Mohammad Iqbal:

1] Where was he born, when?

2] His parents' names.

3] What his parents did. What were they like, if Muneeza remembers.

4] Are they alive? Where?

I realized that I needed to speak to them if they were. Hell, how could I do this story with only one source? Surely that was meant to be just a starting point. What was wrong with me, I wasn't thinking.

5] What school did he go to? English medium or Urdu medium or Hindi medium?

6] Ditto about his wife.

7] Did he play any sports? Did he follow any? Did he like cricket? If so, who was his favourite cricketer?

8] His favourite books? *Don Quixote*, going by Muneeza's anecdote?

9] What kind of husband was he? Did he buy surprise gifts for his wife ever? Did he remember her birthday, anniversary? Did he remember Muneeza's birthday? What were the typical birthday gifts he gave her? Did she still have any of them? And did he give her cards with them?

If so, I needed to see them. Would she show them to me?

10] Did he take her out? Where? For movies? What kind of movies did they see together? What kind of movies did he like?

11] What newspapers did he subscribe to? Did she know which pages he read from them? Sports page first or front page first? Did he read the edits and op-eds?

12] What kind of clothes did he like to wear? What did he wear at home? Was it important for him? Would she go with him when he bought clothes?

13] After her mother died, in what ways did he try to make up for her absence? Did he buy clothes for her? Did he help her with her homework? Was she made to cook, or did he cook, or did he have a maid? How did he cope with her growing-up needs?

How did he help her understand her puberty? **Did she go to him, face scrunched up in that cute way of hers, worried, saying** *Abbu, I'm bleeding*? **But of course I couldn't ask that.**

14] Did they ever speak about her mother? Did he miss her? **(Obviously!)** What signs did he show of this?

15] Does she know if he ever contemplated marrying again?

16] What were his ambitions for her?

17] What were his future plans for himself? Was he happy doing what he did?

18] What exactly did he do? What did his job involve?

19] Was he a strict father? Did she have a curfew to get home by? How did he react to her having male friends?

20] Did he expect to arrange her marriage for her one day? How modern was he? How would he have reacted if she showed up with a lover one day and announced that she wanted to marry him? What if this lover was Hindu?

I stopped here. This was enough for now. I'd take a break, I thought. Some black coffee. Or maybe I'd go out and buy some cans of beer. Maybe I'd watch some television, flip through channels, look for sheer dresses on FTV, maybe a Roberto Cavalli show, or switch between MTV and Channel [V] and VH1, waiting in vain for a song I liked, or just some random action flick on one of the movie channels, with fighting and violence and guns going off and explosions. Maybe.

I knew that many of these questions would never be answered, but I needed to make a list, and then take it from there. But say I got answers to all these questions. Say I got answers to 80 questions more, or 800 questions more, all piercing questions bringing insightful answers. Even then, how much would I really know about this man? I had told Muneeza that I wanted my piece to give 'a sense of this man' to readers — but was it possible for me to get a sense of someone I'd never even met? Did I even have a sense of my own family, my own father, who died when I was 18, and whose last words to me were *'Is the fan on?'* Wasn't there a Mohammad Iqbal who was a stranger even to his own daughter sometimes, who hid smutty magazines in his locked cupboard, who masturbated in the toilet and cried afterwards, who sometimes wished he'd never had the daughter he loved, who was sometimes vicious and mean and not Don Quixote but a murderer in a Maigret novel, mixed-up and confused and a stranger to himself and others in this bewildering world?

Journalism seemed so foolish now, this whole charade of reporting facts when the facts were never enough. But what was the point of being philosophical about it? This wasn't like me. Enough thinking. It was time to get some beer.

I had six cans of beer while watching TV, and a mountain of masala peanuts. Then I slept. I woke up in the middle of the night needing to go to the loo. I had the loosies. I went back to sleep. I woke up again. I was hungry. There was nothing to eat at home. I'd forgotten to buy bread so I couldn't even make myself some toast. I drank some water. There were two cans of beer left. But I couldn't have any more. I went back to bed, and couldn't sleep for the longest time. Then I woke up, and it was nine o'clock, and I was going to be late for my meeting with Muneeza, and I had a headache, and I really didn't want to go, but I had to.

6. Bodybuilding for Dummies

'Hi, sorry, have you been waiting long?'

'No, it's okay.'

'Sorry, sorry, I had a late night, and I woke up late.'

'You were working?'

'Er, no, not exactly.'

'Oh.'

'I'm getting myself a coffee, what would you like to have?'

We sat down five minutes later, coffee at our table, and got to work. I had my notebook open.

'Listen, I realized that the story's progressing too slowly, and I need to be more methodical and just get a lot of basic biographical details to begin with. So I've got a list of questions. You ready?'

She was peering at my notebook. 'Okay.'

Just then the fattest man in India appeared at our table. 'Excuse me, I was sitting here.'

'Sorry?' I said.

'I was sitting here. I just went to get my gelato, and I left my book on the table to reserve it for myself.'

'There's no book on the table.'

'Oh.'

'There,' Muneeza pointed two tables away. 'There's a book on that table.'

'Oh, yes, that is the table. Confusion. I am sorry. Thank you.'

He waddled off to his table and picked up a thick book. The title was *Bodybuilding for Dummies*. Muneeza and I looked at each other and suppressed our laughter.

◂▪

We moved through the list. Birthday, birthplace, check. Parents' names, check. And so on down the list. Muneeza was in a mood to talk, and I wrote furiously. I found many of the details about her father boring. Just as I was gathering the meat for the story, I was losing interest in it. The parts that most interested me were the ones that involved Muneeza.

'So he didn't want you to learn cooking and all the things girls learn.'

'Yes. I mean, it's not like he didn't want me to learn, but he never put pressure on me. My friends in school, there were things they were allowed to do and things they were not allowed to do. Abbu never forced me to do anything. In fact he would encourage me to take part in sports and extra-curricular activities. But I learnt to cook anyway, I enjoyed it. But even when the bai didn't come, he would not let me cook, he would say, you're too young, this is a parent's job.'

'How was his cooking?'

She laughed. 'What to say now? It was okay. But I wasn't fussy. I ate anything he made, and it was always eatable, it was never bad. But I am a better cook! The first time I made a proper meal for him was when I made some dal gosht. That was his favourite dish. On Sundays he would sometimes get food from outside, and he would often get the dal gosht from Noorani. Anyway, I got myself the recipe, took instructions from a friend's mother, and made it for him. It was a surprise for him. It wasn't fantastic, not as good as Noorani, but he was so happy. He was almost bouncing around the house. He wanted to take me out for a film the next day. I said, Abbu, I have school. He said, never mind, you bunk, I will take you for a Govinda film. I said Abbu, no, it's not good to bunk like that. He said, you're right, it's not good, we'll go on Sunday.'

'And he took you for the film?'

'Yes!'

'You like Govinda?'

'I love Govinda. He's such timepass. I love his humour. It's very bad, but, you know...'

'It's very good.'

'Yes!'

◾

We were there till about noon. The fat man with the bodybuilding book finished his gelato slurpaciously and ambled off. Two teenage girls came and sat nearby and giggled over a plate of nachos. A young man sat near a plug point with a laptop and played InkBall. A family of four sat at the next table, looked sad, didn't say a word to one another, ate their food, and left. We spoke and spoke till I was hungry. When our conversation reached a natural lull, and I had asked all I intended to from my list, I suggested that we go for lunch.

'Okay,' she said, and looked around.

'The food court's boring,' I said, 'let's go across the road, there's a terrific Italian restaurant there.'

'Pasta?'

'Yep. It's called Little Italy. The waitresses are all from the North East and the music is American pop from the 80s, but I like the food. Coming?'

'It must be expensive.'

'Not very,' I lied. 'Anyway office pays. Come, come, come.'

We got up and walked towards the escalator. On the way I saw a guy at the ice-cream stand who looked like someone I knew — but it wasn't him. I looked at Muneeza's reflection in a full-length mirror ahead of us. She was dressed in a simple blue salwar-kameez, and her bearing, the way she walked, the way she held her slender frame, was immensely elegant. I didn't feel ashamed of being with her.

∎

We set out to cross the road. The traffic, as usual, was chaotic. I felt like taking her hand and guiding her across.

Just as I thought this, there was a gap in the traffic and she darted across.

Then she stood at the divider, looked at me from across the road, and smiled.

∎

'Would you like a drink?'

'You're going to drink now?'

'No, I mean, iced tea, etc. Why would I drink now?'

'Er, I don't know. Okay, iced tea.'

I called the waiter over. 'Two iced teas, please.'

'Flavour?'

'Peach for me. What about you, Muneeza?'

'The same.'

'Two peach iced teas. We'll order the main course in a minute.'

Muneeza studied the menu. I remembered a recurring dream I used to have as a schoolboy. In the dream, I'd go for my final exam and find that the question paper was written in a language I didn't understand. I'd look around. Everyone else seemed to be managing just fine. Only I didn't understand the language. And then I'd realize that the problem wasn't with the language of the question paper, it was with me: I had forgotten how to read.

'Decided what you want?'

'Why don't you order for me as well? You know what is good here.'

'Sure,' I said. I called the waiter.

We didn't speak much as we waited for our food. Suddenly, after the easy chatter of the morning, we didn't know what to say to each other. We had reached that space where polite small talk seems too contrived. I whipped out my phone at one point and pretended to check my messages. Then I thought that was rude, and I put it away. She fiddled with the sleeve of her kurta. She rearranged the cutlery in front of her. The iced tea arrived, and gave us both something to focus on. We waited for the other person to break the silence, which grew stronger and stronger. Then my phone rang.

'Hello?'

'Abir, this is Mahesh.'

'Hi, Mahesh.'

'Where are you?'

'Er, I'm working on that story.'

'I see. How's it going?'

'Good, good.'

'Are you coming in today?'

'I wasn't planning to, was planning just to work on this. Do you need me for something?'

'Nothing urgent. But come in tomorrow, meeting in my office at noon.'

'Okay. Anything, er, important?'

'Nothing, just be here at noon.'

'Okay.'

He hung up. Rule No. 33 of Corporate Life: Always let the boss hang up first.

'Do you have to go now?'

'No, no, I don't have to go to office today. But I have to be there tomorrow.'

'Okay.'

'Oh, look, our food is coming.'

∎

The pasta on the plate suddenly took female form and started moaning and saying *Ooh, aah, ooh, aah, aah, aaah, aaaah!*

What the fuck are you doing? I asked.

I'm coming, said Pasta Woman. *You said, 'Oh, look, our food is coming.' So I'm coming. Are you happy now, you idiot? Could you think of nothing better to say?*

∎

We didn't speak much while eating either. The restaurant was empty. The waiters were looking at us. Some of them were taking photographs, others were taking notes. Okay, they were not.

'So,' I said, 'why did you say the other day that you don't want to watch a film with me?'

'Because, that's not why we're meeting.'

'Sure, but listen, what's the big deal, we can be friends anyway, right?'

'Ya, okay.'

Ya, okay?

'Which film did you have in mind?' she asked.

'I didn't really think about it.'

'I don't want to see that new Shah Rukh Khan film, I can't stand his acting.'

'Neither can I! All the pigs in India put together don't have that much ham. What about the new Priyadarshan film? That should be timepass.'

'Ya, okay. But I have one condition.'

'What?'

'I'll pay for my own ticket. I'm sure your office doesn't pay for movie tickets also.'

'Sure! But I'll buy you popcorn then. Otherwise my male ego might be hurt.'

She smiled.

◼

The problem with watching a film at a theatre in Bombay is that there are other people around. Don't get me wrong, I'm not a misanthrope. It's just that when I want to watch a movie, I want to *watch a movie*. Many other viewers believe that there are other things to do in a movie hall.

In the seats behind us, for example, a couple were making out. There were two problems with that.

Problem one, they were making noise – not much, but even giggling and heavy breathing can be irritating. A Priyadarshan film is not an intense artistic experience that requires immersion, but still.

Problem two, the guy was sitting right behind me, and kept kicking my chair. This is a common problem at movie halls, and turning around and staring usually does the trick, or politely asking the person to stop if it comes to that.

So at one point, before the interval, I turned around and stared. They continued nibbling each other, which no doubt made my staring seem perverse. So I said, 'Excuse me.'

'Yes.'

The guy glared at me, all alpha male in front of his chica. I was flustered. Instead of saying *'Can you please stop kicking my chair?'* I said:

'Can you please stop doing that?'

The girl giggled. Alpha Male looked at me as if I was insane.

I clarified: 'I mean, stop kicking my chair. That's all. You're kicking my chair. Please stop that. Thanks.'

I turned back around, beginning to sweat despite the AC. The guy tapped my shoulder. Muneeza was staring straight ahead. I turned around.

'I have also paid for ticket,' Alpha Male said, his nose twitching. 'We are paying customer.'

'Yes, but you have bought ticket to watch movie,' I said, 'not to kick my chair.'

'So you watch movie, no. Why you turning around and watching us?'

Muneeza put her hand on my arm. 'Just stop kicking my chair, okay?' I said, and turned back around. Paresh Rawal looked at me from the screen and started laughing.

◾

'Who would have thought you had such a temper?' Muneeza said after the film.

'What do you mean? I've always had a temper.'

'Ya, but when we first met, I thought you were a calm kind of man, I thought I was the emotional one. But every day I learn more and more about you!'

'That's not a good thing. I will attempt to be inscrutable for the rest of the day.'

'You can't. I'm a woman. I see everything.'

'Okay, then tell me what colour underwear I'm wearing.'

'Tchha! You're disgusting.'

'I did offer to be inscrutable.'

◾

We had another coffee, took a quick round of Bookends, and then I offered to drop her home.

'No, it's a long way, I'll take a bus.'

'No, listen, I want to drop you.'

'You don't have to.'

'I want to. Please let me.'

'Okay.'

Where's a fancy car when you need it most? We got into an auto rickshaw, and made our way painfully through traffic. It took one-and-a-half hours to reach her home. I dropped her outside a block of apartments opposite a fire station.

'This is damn far,' I said. 'How long does it take you in the morning to get to Eterniti?'

'About an hour and twenty minutes.'

'You know, I could easily come and meet you somewhere this side, you shouldn't have to travel so far.'

'It's okay. I prefer meeting you there, that's nicer.'

'Okay.'

'Do you have all the information you need?'

'I think so.'

'Oh.'

'Shall we meet tomorrow?'

'Why?'

'So I can practise inscrutability.'

'Listen...'

'Listen, Muneeza.'

'What?'

'Forget why we met. We can be friends. I enjoy spending time with you. We don't only need to meet for work.'

I think I said it too fast.

'Okay.'

'Tomorrow then?'

'What time?'

'I have to go to office in the morning. Why don't I call you? Oh, okay, I can't call you. Can you call me, say around two, and we'll meet in the evening?'

'Okay. I'll call at two.'

'Bye, take care.'

'Bye.'

'Chalo, boss.' This was to the auto driver. The machine started moving. Muneeza turned and walked towards her home.

◼

Why did I want to be friends with her? We had nothing in common – and I'm not just talking about class or religion. We had nothing to talk about. We listened to different kinds of music, we read different books, I hated bloody Govinda – though it's cool to like him, like Lalu Prasad Yadav, so that's what I pretend. We couldn't even discuss food while we had our lunch. We probably had completely different ways of looking at the world. I couldn't just 'hang out' with Muneeza and 'shoot the breeze'. So why did I want to meet her again?

In the red corner, Heart. In the blue corner, Brain. The bell rings. Brain steps out and weaves about in a cerebral manner, footwork assured, technique impeccable. Heart saunters out, belches, and swings wildly. A few second later, Brain is on the floor, trying to breathe. Heart, like a WWF wrestler, climbs onto the ropes at the side of the ring and dives onto Brain, elbow first. Brain goes into coma. Heart raises arms, triumphant over an enemy that never had a chance in the first place.

7. When Lives Collide

When I walked into office the next morning it felt just a little bit unfamiliar. You know how you get used to something – your workplace, or your neighbourhood, or the taste of a dish you eat often – and then you don't really notice it, you take it for granted. And then suddenly one day you notice it again, and see it in a new light. Well, that's what happened to me now.

My desk was dingy and cluttered; the corridors, lit by blue light even during the day, were depressing; the people all looked sad, even though a fat girl called Mohini who didn't wear bras on principle was laughing obscenely near the pantry – she caught me looking at her disgusting wobbling breasts and raised an amused eyebrow. I walked off to my desk, wondering if I should send her an email to clarify the situation – 'I wasn't looking at them with lust, you cow, but with horror.'

I checked my email, glanced at all my favourite websites – India Uncut hadn't been updated for 48 hours; bastard! – and then, with 20 minutes still left for the noon meeting, walked over to chat with D'Souza. I think I get this trait of sadomasochism from my mother – after all, she had me.

I peered into his cubicle, where he was busy typing something. 'Good morning, sir.'

'Ah. Abir. Good morning to you as well. Of what service can I be to you? Should I get you a cup of tea, perhaps? Tell me how much sugar you like.'

'I just came over to say hi.'

'Your kindness is astonishing. I am blessed.'

Then I suppose he realized that he was overdoing it. He slipped into human mode, and his voice dropped a register.

'Everything okay?'

'Yes, sir, everything's fine.'

'How's your story going?'

'It's going okay. Mahesh called me for a meeting at 12, so I came for that.'

'Ah, of course, yes. All the best.'

'Thank you, sir.'

I walked away, thinking how surreal this was. D'Souza and I had lapsed into politeness with each other. The next thing I knew Mohini would start wearing bras and write to her parents saying, '*I just*

realized I am 38, and my whole life has been a mistake.
Please arrange a marriage for me. P.S. I know I'm not
a virgin so maybe you could look for a divorcee?'

◆

'Abir, meet Sandhya Kirloskar. Sandhya is your
new boss.'

'Oh, Mahesh, don't say "boss". I hate that
word,' said Sandhya in a husky voice. 'Abir, pleased
to meet to you, we'll be working together on *The
Mumbaikar*.'

'Hi. The... Mumbaikar?'

'Yes,' said Mahesh. 'That's the new name of our
new supplement. Sandhya will be the editor of *The
Mumbaikar*, and I'm shifting you to work for her
now. From today, you report to her. You're off the
crime beat.'

'Oh.'

'She's officially joining us from Monday, but for
all practical purposes she's taking over operational
charge from today. I've told her about the stories
that I've already commissioned – which didn't take
long, as there are just three of them. But yours is
the biggest, and should be our first cover story.'

'I'm very excited about it,' Sandhya said. 'It's
the sort of story that the best feature writers in
the industry would be glad to sink their teeth into.

Mahesh has very good things to say about you, and I'm looking forward to seeing what you deliver.'

'Thanks. I'm, um, really glad to get this chance. I'm going to give you something kickass.'

'Fantastic,' said Mahesh. 'Let me tell you what your role in the supplement will be once you're done with this. A – you'll be a feature writer, but writing on subjects like crime and city issues rather than entertainment or celebrities or other soft issues. B – you'll also have page-making responsibilities, as you did when you first joined this paper. C – we'd like you to do a weekly diary of events in the city as covered by us. We'll run your photograph with it, so you might need to get a haircut soon.'

I'd been planning to get a haircut anyway.

'That sounds amazing. I'm sure I'll have fun.'

'Fun is the right word,' said Sandhya. 'I like my team to think of work as fun. That's when great journalism happens.'

She gave me a plastic smile. I gave her a plastic smile back.

◼

Fifteen minutes later Sandhya and I were sitting in an empty cabin in a corner of the office which was to become her workspace. She'd said she wanted to discuss the story with me, so I debriefed her on what I'd gathered so far. I told her about Mohammad Iqbal, the kind of biographical details I'd gathered, and tried to give her a sense of the story I would weave out of it, which I wasn't even sure of myself. She heard me out, then drawled:

'Abir, that sounds just fantastic. I'm looking forward to it a lot. I have a couple of small suggestions, though, yours to deal with as you please.'

'Tell me.'

'What was the name of the police officer who led the team that shot this Iqbal fellow? I believe you know him, since you've been on the crime beat.'

'Er, Vallabh Thombre. Yes, I know him.'

'Do you like him? Is he a good guy?'

'Er, I know him on a professional basis, really, but he seems nice enough.'

'Good. What I was thinking was, what about converting this story into a dual profile? On one hand, you write about Mohammad Iqbal. On the other, you write about this police officer. Write about both their lives, sort of in parallel. Humanize them both. Involve the readers in both their lives, make the readers root for both of them, leave them conflicted in the end. That'll bring out the complexities of the issues involved. In 3000 words, you'll tell a story of two men whose lives collide in the city of Bombay.'

Whose lives collide in the city of Bombay. It sounded like a blurb for a book. I was worried now. I didn't want to do a story on Thombre. For one, if the story made an impact, a media focus on him could get me into trouble. After all, I was there that night.

'Well, that… sounds great. But actually the story is already working out to be quite substantial, and I'm not sure we need another element to it.'

'I know, I know, you've been working hard on it. I'm not saying I want you to abandon your plans for the story and take this up. It's just a suggestion. But do take some time and think about it. Personally, I think it could make for a richer, deeper story.'

'I'll think about it.'

'Thank you. And remember, it's your call, I'm just making a suggestion.'

◾

I'm just making a suggestion. Now, what was that code for? I didn't know this woman, this Shobha De lookalike in her starched maroon sari, well enough to know if she was just into suggesting or if, in her editorial stylesheet, 'suggestion' meant 'order'. If it was a suggestion, I would ignore it. If it was an order, I would have to do it. Or I'd have to come up with good enough reasons not to. Such as?

One, I could argue that doing a story that implied that Thombre killed a man in cold blood would make me lose access to my sources, which is disastrous for any reporter. But that wouldn't work: firstly, I wasn't on the crime beat anymore; secondly, as she would know if she had any experience in newsrooms, our paper wouldn't lose access either because the cops gain as much from cultivating reporters as vice versa.

Two, I could take a principled stand, saying that by treating Iqbal and Thombre equally, we were implying a moral equivalence between the two men. But if Sandhya had any sense, she would laugh me out of the room, if not my job, if I made this argument. Firstly, reporters aren't supposed to make value judgements. Secondly, what does journalism have to do with principles? Seriously...

Three, I could show her a draft of my story as I saw it, as per Mahesh's original brief, and it would be so kickass that she would be loathe to chop it up into half and dilute its impact. But this was wishful thinking. If Sandhya had already made up her mind on how she wanted the story, nothing would persuade her otherwise. She'd prefer a mediocre story on both men than a great story on one man, and she'd rationalize that mediocrity superbly, drawling huskily. I wouldn't have a chance.

So what to do? I'd figure it out later: my phone was ringing.

It was Muneeza. She didn't sound her normal self.

'You sound tired,' I said. 'Is everything okay?'

'Ya. I mean... okay. I'll tell you when we meet.'

'What time?'

'Five o'clock?'

'Cool. You want me to come to your side of town?'

'No, no, Eterniti is better.'

'Eterniti then.'

'Bye.'

I got there 10 minutes late and found Muneeza in Bookends, browsing through an issue of *Elle*. We went and got coffee for me and iced tea for her and sat in a relatively quiet corner. Two tables away, a disgusting teenage boy pawed a disgusting teenage girl. Both of them, I thought, were surplus to the workings of the universe. Muneeza didn't seem to notice them.

'How was your meeting?' she asked.

'My what? Oh, meeting. It was cool. Routine office work. I have a new boss. She looks like Shobha De. Or

Shobhaa-aa-aa-aa De, whatever her name is these days after her latest meeting with her numerologist.'

Muneeza looked serious. My attempt at levity hadn't worked. 'You tell me, what's happening? Did you resume college today?'

'No. I thought I'd start tomorrow. I wish I'd gone today itself.'

'Something happened at home?'

'I fought with my aunt.'

'Oh.'

'I told you about her, na. She's very orthodox and strict. My father disliked her. He would have been horrified to have found I'm staying with her.'

'What did you fight about?'

'Well, just my whole life. She's not happy with the way I dress, she says it was okay when I was 15, but I need to be more proper now that I'm old enough.'

'Old enough for what?'

'For men to look at me. You know the thinking.'

'Ouch. I do.'

'Anyway, so she got upset about why I'm going off to meet you again. She said it's not good to meet a boy like this every day.' Muneeza raised her eyebrows. 'I had told her about the story you are doing. Today she said, why bother, what good will come from it, let it rest.

'So I told her, anyway, the story part is over, I'm just going to meet him because he's a friend. And she started nagging. She said, "What would your father have thought?" That's when I got angry. I felt like telling her what my father thought of her. But I couldn't do that, as I'm staying with her. So she feels she can run my life, and make me do things her way.'

'Which is?'

'Which is, get married soon, have many children, and so on. I don't want all that. I'll feel like I have died if that happens, especially if I have an arranged marriage with whoever my aunt chooses. Abbu would not have wanted me to do all that. He would have wanted me to be independent. But here I am, stuck in this situation.'

'You really can't go back to your old home?'

'No.'

'So what are your options?'

'First I'll go to my college and see if they have a vacancy in the hostel. I doubt it, but I'll try. I'll find out about other girls hostels. In a few months I'll graduate, and I'll give MBA entrance exams. If I get through somewhere, I'll try for a scholarship or a loan. If I don't get that, I'll manage on my father's savings until I finish my MBA, and then I'll be independent.'

'Er, you make it sound very easy, but getting into one of the good MBA colleges takes a bit of doing.'

'I can do it. If I know what to aim for and I work hard, I can do anything.'

'Cool,' I said. 'Then that sounds like a good plan. But what if you don't get a hostel now? You're going to continue to stay with your aunt?'

'No. I have to find something.'

I dropped her home again. I didn't have to offer to do so, and she didn't ask why we were getting into an auto together. We both had worries somewhat greater than protocol.

◢◣

It was just after eight when I dropped her off. As the auto made its return journey, I called Thombre.

'Ganguly,' said Thombre. 'How are things? I tried calling two days back, we solve kidnapping case, phone on voicemail. Then Hegde told you're not on crime beat anymore.'

'That's right, I got shifted to this new supplement the paper is starting.'

'So you will cover Page 3 parties? Ha ha ha ha.'

'No, I'll be doing features and all. Actually, Thombresaab, I had some work with you regarding a story I'm doing, can I drop in and see you sometime?'

'Why not? You want to come now?'

'Are you very busy now?'

'I'm on duty, but we can have chai.'

'Actually, I needed to sit and talk with you for a bit longish period of time, at least half an hour or so.'

'Okay. Then why don't we meet tomorrow. I need to be at work at 11, so let's meet at 10.30 before that?'

'Cool. I'll come to the police station?'

'Meet me at station. We will go for tea.'

'Okay. Thanks a lot. I'll see you tomorrow.'

8. The Real Mohammad Iqbal

By now I was getting used to waking up early. I was up 10 minutes before the alarm rang, waiting for it to ring so I could 'Stop!' instead of 'Snooze'. I felt alert, ready to take on the world, leave alone an alarm clock, ready to sit up and solve 18 sudokus in two minutes.

The alarm rang. 'Ha!' I said loudly, and slapped it. Then I closed my eyes and went back to sleep.

■

'Ganguly, there you are. You are late.'

'Sorry, Thombresaab, I was working till 4am, you know how it is in newspapers, I overslept.'

'Never mind, Gangulys are always late. That cricketer fellow, ha ha ha.'

'Ha ha. Have I come too late or do you have time for a chai?'

'For you, Ganguly, I will always have time. Criminals can wait. Ha ha ha.'

He was in a jolly mood. He barked some instructions to his havaldar – mundane ones, nothing like *Get the boiling oil ready for the prisoner, I'll be back soon with a battleaxe* – and we trotted over to the chai-shed.

'Tell me, how this humble police officer can help you?'

'Thombresaab, a few days ago, my editor called me in and asked me to do a story. Basically... you remember that night I came with you and you guys shot a man named Mohammad Iqbal? Well, my boss asked me to do a story on him.'

'What kind of story? That man was criminal, died in encounter with police, happen all the time.' The mood had changed.

'No, not an encounter story. They just wanted a story on his life, showing the person he was, etc., without going into details of how he died. A profile. Well, anyway, my editor has now suggested that I also do a profile of you side by side. The man who was shot and the man who led the team that shot him.'

'I don't understand, why? What will story say? He was innocent and I killed him?'

'No, no. Their idea – see, this is not my idea, I'm just following orders – their idea is that we do stories of both you and him, make the audience see your point of view and sympathize with both people, and make them feel, er, ambivalent about the shooting.'

'But why? See, Iqbal was criminal, he deserve to die. How can you treat criminal equally with police officer like me, doing duty?'

'But, er, you're sure he was such a criminal? See, I've been talking to his daughter and his employer...'

'Arre baba, you know me for long time, would I make mistake? He was with Chhota Sion gang. He used to do accounts. They had two accountant people, he was one, other is in jail. He will tell you same thing that I am saying now.'

'But he had a job at an NGO.'

'That was just cover, Ganguly. How much would NJO pay him? Ten thousand, fifteen thousand? How far that goes in Bombay? He had grown-up daughter to bring up, he was renting flat in Mahalaxmi. Fine, not fancy society, but still, Mahalaxmi. You find out rent and expenses, you see salary. I'm telling you, not possible with NJO job.'

'NGO. But why did you have to shoot him? He didn't even have a gun.'

'I'm saying he did. I am lying?'

He was breathing heavily now. He paused. He gulped down his tea.

'Look, Ganguly, you are friend, so I'm telling you. Maybe we overreacted. Maybe. But he was member of that gang, for sure. When police go to arrest gang, sometime this happen. It is not unusual. It is risky to fight gangs.'

In school my nickname was 'Gangs'. I nodded. We finished our tea.

'You want to do story, Ganguly, do story,' said Thombre. 'But remember that you are side of law and order. After all, you were also with me that night.'

We got up, I was about to pay when I realized who I was with and put my wallet back in my pocket.

'And Ganguly, if you're sending photographer, tell in advance, I will get some good clothes out. Okay?' He was cheerful again.

'Okay,' I said.

◾

I went to office. I was confused. If I hadn't met Muneeza, if nothing had happened between the shooting and now, I'd have taken Thombre at his word. After all, he's a well-regarded cop with a tough job. If he says Mohammad Iqbal was a gangster, well, why should I disbelieve him? But now I knew Muneeza, and I'd seen pictures of Iqbal at his wedding, and he was no longer a stranger. The two Mohammad Iqbals here, Thombre's Iqbal and

Muneeza's Iqbal, didn't go together. Could they be the same person?

I walked over to Mohan's desk. He was sitting with a new trainee girl called Preeti, who looked 12. He was telling her about some film he'd just seen.

'And do you know what happens after her head gets cut off?'

'What?' asked Preeti, with a look of both horror and fascination on her face.

'These urchins in the forest, they take her head and play football with it. One side scores a goal. They all celebrate. That's the last scene of the film. What a fantastic scene!'

'Um-hmm.'

'Anyway, so I was saying, are we on for lunch on Sunday, and a movie after that?'

'Er, I'll have to see. I just realized I might have a family engagement, it's my aunt's birthday.'

'How old will she be?'

'I don't know. It's not polite to ask, no?'

'Well, okay. Let me know if you happen to be free, I've downloaded some supercool films. I don't even mind watching *Hostel 2* again.'

'Okay.' Preeti gave me a weak smile as she walked off, no doubt telling herself that she needed to watch a few episodes of *Scooby Doo* to forget what Mohan had just told her.

'So how's life, dude? How's your story going?'

'It's going okay. It's complicated. Not an easy story. How're things with you?'

'Same old, same old. I'm getting a bit sick of this job, to be honest. I've started working out at a gym.'

'Eh?'

'Yes, I thought I'll try my hand out at acting or something. Have you seen all these TV actors? Dude, every time I eat out I bump into one of them, and they're all so short and ordinary-looking and all.'

'That's true.'

'Not to mention inarticulate and stupid. Not what they seem on TV at all.'

'I'll take your word for it.'

'You're laughing at me, aren't you?'

'No yaar, why should I laugh? I hope you succeed and get your ass out of this sordid place.'

'You're laughing at me. You're thinking, this joker wants to be an actor. Ha ha, he can never be an actor. But you're thinking that because you've seen the subeditor side of me. When people see the acting side of me, they'll wonder how I could ever have been a subeditor. Like people who see Akshay Kumar and wonder how he was ever a waiter.'

'Actually, when I see Akshay Kumar, I wonder why he still isn't a waiter.'

'Eh?'

'But no, dude, I'm sure you'll do well.' I reached out and touched his biceps. He flinched and moved his arm away.

'I've just joined, dude,' he said. 'Wait a few weeks.'

I didn't call people 'dude' before I met Mohan. But since we became friends, I'm always 'dude this' and 'dude that'. That's simply because he keeps calling me (and everyone else, including his dudewallah) dude, and I've picked up his lingo. I adapt to the people around me at any given moment, as I guess everyone does.

So who were the people who were around Mohammad Iqbal in his life, whom he adapted to? One way to find out, at least as far as the last few years were concerned, was to speak to Meenakshi. She had been his boss, and I wanted to know what she had to say about him. I called her up and fixed a meeting. 'Is four o'clock okay with you?' she asked. 'Certainly,' I said, and cancelled all my pending appointments for the day. Heh.

Meenakshi had a busy look about her when I reached her office, but she didn't actually seem to be doing anything. She sat me down and asked the peon to get me some black coffee. The peon gave me a surly look.

'You son of a bitch,' he said, 'when people ask for coffee I just give them that normal crap from the old machine we have, with too much milk and sugar. But if they want black coffee, I have to spend 10 minutes heating water and all. I hate you. I spit on your family. I will copulate with your pet puppy, if you have one.'

Okay, he didn't say this. But I'm good at reading minds.

'So tell me, Abir, have you written your story yet?'

'I'm working on it. I've, um, met Muneeza a few times, got to know a lot about her father. And I was hoping to chat about him with you as well, to get a better sense of the guy.'

'Yes, sure. What would you like to know?'

'Well, to begin with, how did you first meet him? And what made you offer him a job?'

'Oh, this was, let me see, 11 years ago now. This was a few months before we started Teach Your Children. I used to work as an activist at that time in an NGO called Justice Denied, and we were following up on the case of a builder's murder in

Bhandup. There was pressure on the police to solve the case, and they had arrested five men from there, all Muslims, and one of them committed suicide in prison. I first met Iqbal around that time. He came to speak to us about the case. He was a friend of a couple of those men, and he told us that they were innocent, and that one of them had been out of town at the time of the murder, and another had been with him at the time. He seemed a decent fellow, educated and so on, so we decided to look into the case. We even got your newspaper to carry a story about the lack of evidence, and how implausible the police account of things was.'

'And then?'

'And then a couple of gangsters got arrested after a shootout somewhere else, and they confessed to this murder. It was clear that these five guys had been arrested because the police needed to show that it was doing its job, that it was efficient. Well, once the real culprits were released, the police let these men go. Except the guy who'd died, obviously.'

'So was there much of a fuss about this in the papers?'

'Of course there was. The newspapers carried stories on it for, let me see, about a week. Then they stopped and moved on to some other sensational stories. What did they care about some poor Muslim lower-class man somewhere? If the victims had been middle-class like you or me, then there might have been a hue and cry. See, Abir, you're a journalist, you know: "Miscarriage of justice" makes for a good story; "Nothing done about miscarriage of justice" can also run on the inside pages; but after that, "Still nothing done about miscarriage of justice after two weeks" is not a story anymore, it's boring. Go on, give us something new, the readers think. And can you blame them?'

'So anyway, that's when you met Iqbal?'

'Yes, he was a good man, soft-spoken and obviously intelligent, and I found out while chatting with him that he was an accountant. A friend and I were then thinking of starting this organization, and I found that Iqbal was then out of work. I asked him for his qualifications, they seemed decent, so I offered him a job. He was with us since then.'

'One question: are you absolutely sure that the five men arrested then were innocent?'

'Of course! The gangsters arrested later confessed!'

'Yes, but maybe the cops made them confess because the heat was on them regarding these five guys, because you guys were on their case.'

Meenakshi paused, as if this was the first time that possibility had crossed her mind. 'Look, anything is possible, but I'm pretty sure those five men were innocent. I can't remember the details now, but we looked into the details, and at the police allegations, and it was clear that they were being framed. Completely clear.'

'See, I'll tell you where I'm coming from. I've met Muneeza a few times and got a very positive picture of her father. But I happened to meet the inspector who shot Muneeza's father today morning. He is convinced that Iqbal was part of an underworld gang, that his work for you was just a front. I really don't know what to think...'

'Abir, that's outrageous. The man who murdered him will obviously say he was part of a gang. Obviously! In all these years, no cop has ever stood up and said in so many words: "Look, we made a mistake, sorry." You really need to take everything the police say with a pinch of salt.'

'Okay, okay. Look, I'm not saying I believed him, but he threw these points up, and I thought I need to find out more.'

'What points?'

'Well, to start with, he found it implausible that Iqbal could have rented the flat he did in Mahalaxmi on the salary he must have had. What was his salary, by the way?'

'I don't know if I should... Okay, what the hell, we paid him about 22 thousand a month.'

'Twenty-two thousand!'

She misunderstood my exclamation. 'He was very competent,' she said.

'No, I'm just wondering, isn't that too little to manage on in Bombay?'

'Abir, how much do you earn?'

'I make more than that, and despite being a bachelor and all, I barely get by.'

'Yes, but you're different. People like Iqbal have a different lifestyle. They manage expenses, they never eat out, they don't buy unnecessary things, they're frugal. I don't know how much he paid as rent, maybe his flat was rent-controlled, I don't know, but I'm sure he would have managed just fine. Look, I know the man, he was a good man, a hard-working man, a decent man. I'm telling you, trust me, he was not a gangster.'

Just then my phone rang. It was Muneeza. Had it been anyone else, I would have said that I was in a meeting, that I'd call back. But Muneeza didn't have a mobile phone where I could call back, so I excused myself and took the call.

'Hi, Muneeza.'

'Abir, hi, you asked me to call so we can fix up a time to meet. Is seven okay? Same place?'

'Er, yes, seven is great. What's the matter, you sound tense, is everything okay?'

'Yes... I mean, I'll tell you when we meet. Seven then, Eterniti.'

'Yep, see you then.'

I hung up. Meenakshi asked: 'That was Muneeza you were speaking to?'

'Yes.'

'Are you meeting her today? Can you tell her to give me a call? I've been trying to call her – her father's things, what he had in his drawers, are all packed in a couple of packets. I need to know if she wants them or...'

'I'll tell her.'

'Thanks. Would you like another cup of coffee?'

We chatted about Muneeza's father for about 40 minutes. Iqbal was a soft-spoken man. He was punctual. He was loyal to Teach Your Children: once, when their funding got delayed, he went without his salary for two months.

'I had told him not to pay my salary but to pay everyone else's,' Meenakshi said, 'but I later found that he himself hadn't drawn a salary during those two months, till the funds came in. I asked him why he did that. He said, "Ma'am, this is my organization also."'

'He was hired initially as an accountant, but he more or less became the main office manager in those years. He would maintain all the files, keep the records. When we got computers and decided to move all our work on the computer and minimize the use of paper, he worked late to supervise the typists we hired to do some of the digitizing of data. My partner Savita, who started this organization with me, left about seven years ago and went abroad with her husband. Since then I've run it alone. Iqbal was like my right hand, he kept the office organized and took care of a lot of the basic details of the job.'

'And what did he talk about outside of work? I mean, did you chat about other things, his personal life, and so on?'

'Abir, here's the thing, and I've been thinking about it for the last few days. He was with me for 11 years. I trusted him completely. I liked him a lot. And yet, in 11 years of working in the same office every day, we never had lunch or dinner together. Not even once.'

She paused, tapped the table.

'What does that say about me? You know, today you can ask me questions about what kind of a person he was, and outside of how he did his office work, I don't have the slightest idea. I feel horrible, *horrible* about that. We activists talk about class differences and class bias and so on, and there is simply no other explanation for why I never had lunch with him. I ate lunch in my cabin or went out to meet friends from the same middle-class background as me, but here was my co-worker for all these years... Anyway, why am I telling you this? I'm becoming a sanctimonious old woman, and I won't even spare myself!'

I looked down, embarrassed at having witnessed her in a private moment. We got back to talking about Iqbal, but none of the things she told me added any insight to what he was all about. After spending time with Muneeza, I felt like I had gotten to know her father as well, and not just in the sense that I asked her questions and she gave me answers. As Meenakshi rebuked herself, I silently rebuked myself for having almost believed Thombre this morning, about Iqbal being a gangster. Iqbal, I concluded, was a good man who worked too hard at his job, from Meenakshi's account, to lead a double life. My feelings about Iqbal were no longer ambivalent – but my article was expected to be.

9. Not The Incredible Hulk

Muneeza was sitting outside Eterniti Mall on the steps at the entrance. She had a large duffel bag with her.

'I didn't want to go inside because the security wanted to check my bag,' she said. 'I didn't want them going through my clothes.'

'Your clothes?'

'Yes. I fought with my aunt. I can't stay there anymore. So I took my things and left.'

'Oh. So where are you going then?'

'I was going to come and meet you anyway, so I thought I'd meet you, and then I'd go to Sonal's house. Remember I told you about Sonal, my college friend?'

'Yep. Where does she live?'

'In Thane.'

'Thane? It'll take you two hours just to get there at this time. You'll get there late at night. Anyway, I'll drop you there. Is Sonal expecting you?'

'I haven't told her yet. I was on my way here, I didn't want to stop in the middle and phone. I thought I'd see you and borrow your mobile phone.'

'Of course. What's her number?'

She gave me Sonal's number, I dialled and handed the phone to her, she walked away to a side. After a while she walked back to me.

'It says her mobile is unavailable.'

'Ah.'

'I know where she lives, so I'll just go there. She's a good friend. Her mother likes me. It won't be a problem.'

'What if she's not at home? What if she's not in town?'

'Where will she go? You don't have to come if you don't want to. I can go on my own.'

'Arre, if she's there of course I'll drop you. But there's no point going all the way and reaching a dead end. Listen, let's go and have a coffee or an early dinner or something, and try calling after half an hour. Hopefully she'll pick up the phone then. If she is I'll drop you there. Thane is beautiful by night.'

'Is it?'

'Of course not.'

We went to Kailash Parbat nearby and I ordered Kasuri Methi Chhole Bhature, hyping it up so much that she ordered the same. 'You've written your story?' she asked.

'No, but I rescued 18 infants today from a global infant sacrifice syndicate and won a million dollars in the world online poker championships.'

'What?'

'I mean, no, it's not easy to write stories like this. Though I do have to finish it by the end of this week. I've just been doing my research so far. I'll probably sit and start writing the first draft tonight or tomorrow morning.'

Then I remembered Thombre, and that the story Muneeza thought I was writing was now just half the story.

'Actually, er, I'll have to do some more research. The deadline seems very tight now.'

'What research?'

'Er, regarding the police, you know...' How could I have told her that I'd be devoting as much newsprint to her father's murderer as to her dad?

'It's not too spicy, is it?'

'What?'

'The Kasturi Methi Chhole Bhature.'

'Kasuri. Of course not. It's gorgeous. If it was a woman I'd marry it.'

'Your children would be kachoris then.'

'That's possible. I'd ask their mother, "Has Chintu come back from school today?" And she'd say, "No, his classmates ate him."'

'You'll name your son Chintu?'

'Of course not. What a horrible name! If my parents had called me Chintu I would have disowned them.'

'So what is your nickname then?'

'Actually it's much worse than Chintu. I'm Bengali. You don't ask Bengali boys their nickname. It is the source of their greatest shame.'

'Tell me your nickname.'

'What did I just tell you?'

'Tell me your nickname!'

'Oh, shut up. Ah, there comes our food.'

◾

'So what happened with your aunt?'

'It's a long story.' Pause.

'It's okay, you don't need to tell me. I under-stand.'

'I'll you the details some other time. But basically I need to get on with my life. That is what Abbu would have wanted also. He hated my aunt.'

'So what's the plan then?'

'Well, I didn't plan this.' She gave me a weak smile. 'I'll just stay with Sonal for a few days, and look for hostel accommodation. Even if my college hostel doesn't have a vacancy, I'll find some other hostel.'

'You don't want to go back home, where you used to live?'

'I told you that day: no!'

'I know, sorry...'

'I mean, I thought about it, but it's too difficult.'

'What about your things?'

'I don't have so many things. I can take them with me. I'll go back one day with Sonal and pack everything. Maybe Sunday.'

'What about furniture and all?'

'I'll find a way to dispose of it. There's not much, and it's old. I don't have any sentimental attachment to the furniture. A bed is just a block of wood. I have enough time till the lease runs out to think what to do.'

'Fair enough.'

'Did you bring a lot of things with you when you came to Bombay?'

'No, hardly. I just got my clothes and some of my books, that's all. I'll probably shift the rest of my books sometime. I hardly need more than that.'

'Exactly.'

'But I know they're there.'

'Sir, tea-coffee-dessert?'

We had finished eating five minutes ago, and now the waiter was standing on our heads. His left foot was on my head, his right foot on Muneeza's, and he wobbled.

■

Muneeza kept calling Sonal, but she couldn't get through. She looked like she was going to cry. Plan A wasn't working out, and there was no Plan B. Maybe I could come up with one.

'Listen, I have a suggestion.'

'What?'

'Come to my place for tonight, and tomorrow you can...'

'No, I can't do that!'

'Listen, don't be silly. I have a 1 BHK, and I sleep on the mattress in the hall, most days anyway, I drift off to sleep watching TV. You can sleep in the bedroom. It's only for one night.'

'I can't do that.'

'Muneeza, you're a friend, you need a place to stay for the night, I happen to have a spare mattress in another room. It's not a big deal. You come on over, and tomorrow you can go find Sonal and enquire about your hostel and whatever you want.'

'Maybe she's watching a movie, so her phone is off, that happens sometime. I'll try again after half an hour.'

This was exasperating. 'Okay, you try after half an hour. But why don't we do one thing? Let's go to my house, we'll relax and watch some TV, I'll make you my Abir Ganguly special coffee, non-decaf, and we'll call Sonal after half an hour, and one hour, and so on. The moment you get to speak to her, we'll head off towards Thane. But if you can't get in touch with her, at least you have a place to stay. Or would you rather go back to your aunt?'

'No.'

'Come along then. And oh, did I tell you I was gay?'

'You're gay?'

'No baba, just joking. Come on now.' I hailed an auto. The driver took one look at me, sneered, and sped off. But I am a man, that's what I am, and eventually I found an auto all right.

◪

My house was a mess, as it always is: some mornings I wake up and have trouble finding myself. Abir, Abir, I shout, as I go from room to room. No success. Then I go through the day feeling disjointed, and when I finally do find myself, it's when I wasn't looking. Whatever.

'Has your mother ever been here?'

'I know what you mean. Er, she visited once when she was going through Bombay, and I tidied up just for her. She still managed to tidy up some more. If you put her in a desert she'll flatten the dunes.'

'No, that's not what I meant at all! It's a nice flat. It doesn't overlook the road and it's quiet.'

'That it is. Do you want some coffee? I'm going to make coffee for myself.'

'Okay, thanks. I think I'll call again now.'

'Sure.'

I handed her my phone and entered the kitchen to heat water. There was a lizard on the wall. It looked at me and said:

'What the fug, Abir, you're getting women in the house now? Do I not do it for you anymore? Do I not get it up, boy?'

'No, it's not that, you misunderstand,' I said.

'Let me ask you one question: Can she crawl on walls? Eh? Can she? Can she fight with monster cockroaches and then eat them? Eh? Can she?'

'You're being too sensitive here. She's just a friend. She needs a place to stay for the night. That's all.'

'That's what they all say. You better behave, that's all, I'm warning you.'

'Fuck you.'

'Fuck you too. I'm going to drop on you guys if you get up to any hanky-panky, I'm warning you now.'

'Heh. Keep watching and waiting then.'

Just then Muneeza walked in and told me that she still couldn't get through to Sonal. And the water went *Hisssssssss...*

'You have many books,' Muneeza said. 'There are a couple I'll borrow from you later.'

'Sure. Books are what I spend most of my money on, actually. Books and eating out.'

'You don't have a maid to come and cook for you?'

'Well, not for cooking. I have a maid for other stuff like cleaning and washing the dishes and washing my clothes. But she's been on a two-week vacation for three weeks now. If she doesn't turn up soon I'll look for another maid.'

'So you've been washing your clothes yourself?'

'No, laundry.'

'That must be very expensive.'

'Yes, but it's a temporary thing. At some point my maid will come back or I'll get another maid. You're scaring me, you know, you're talking like my mother. That's not a good thing.'

'Sorry! I didn't mean to nag.'

'No, I'm kidding.'

'Let me try calling again.'

She went out to the balcony. She was back after a minute.

'No luck?'

She shook her head.

'Well, we don't have an option then. Let me show you the bedroom, I suggest you sleep there. I'll sleep in the hall, maybe I'll work at night.' My bedroom was tiny, and my computer and my TV were both in the hall.

'Listen, I don't want to impose on you...'

'Don't be silly, you're not imposing. The Incredible Hulk is imposing. Let me quickly clear up my bed inside.'

◾

She shut the bedroom door and went to bed. I didn't check if she had locked it from inside. If she had, I might have been offended. If she hadn't, she might have wondered why I was checking. I didn't know her well enough to know what was going through her mind, and I just wanted her to be comfortable. The last few days must have been hellish for her, and even this, staying overnight at the house of a boy she had met just a handful of days ago, must seem so surreal. I wanted to help her get back to normal, with a place to stay and a routine she could absorb herself in. The quicker her life got a rhythm and regularity to it, the quicker she'd get over this and get on with things.

And what was my interest in all of this? I didn't have an answer to that. I liked her and I wanted to help her. I guess that was all.

For the moment.

I worked on the story till about four in the morning. One of the problems while writing a piece like this, I've since realized, is that you get too ambitious. You read your New Journalism pieces from the books where they are collected, you read the features in *The New Yorker* and *The Atlantic*, and you tell yourself you want to write like that, and you paralyze yourself. The trick is just to tell the story simply, the best you can, without thinking of how impressed people will be when they read it. So I wrote and wrote. Muneeza's dad was half the story now, and in my mind I downgraded it from a classic 6000-word profile into half of a 3000-word story. All these days, as I'd been finding out more and more about him, I'd been formulating paragraphs here and there, some with anecdotes, some with straight narrative, some with my own speculation. I wrote all that down.

When I eventually went to bed, I had more than enough on Mohammad Iqbal. The material would need chopping and polishing, but I had it all down. That left the task of meeting Thombre again and getting his story. I figured that would be easier.

Until a couple of days ago, this story had been my biggest immediate problem. Now it was trivial. My problem was what came after. I was a protagonist in the sequel that would never be written, and I had no idea how it would go.

10. 'Everything is Power System'

In my dream I was playing cricket for India. We were playing Pakistan, and their fastest bowler was bowling at me. It was Thombre.

I took guard. Thombre sprinted in. Thombre leaped in the air. I realized that I wasn't wearing my guard. Thombre chucked ferociously. I shut my eyes and covered my crotch. The ball whizzed past.

And then 90,000 people at Eden Gardens laughed at me. Ha Ha Ha Ha Ha, they all went.

■

That's when I woke up. Despite the humiliation in my dream, my morning glory was glorious. I squinted at the clock. Eight-thirty. What was I doing in the hall?

Then I heard the sound of running water in the bathroom and remembered Muneeza. I sat, I blinked,

I stood up. I adjusted my crotch. Then I remembered Eden Gardens.

'I'm glad I warned you,' the lizard said. It eyed me smugly from the wall. 'Otherwise God knows what would have happened.'

■

'I think I'll make some tea for myself,' Muneeza said. 'Would you like some?'

'Sorry, I don't keep tea in the house. I don't drink tea.'

'Oh.'

'Would you like some coffee?'

'Well, okay, but let me make it?'

'Okay. Er, I have it black.'

'I know.'

■

'Sonal's still not picking up her phone.'

'Damn. So what's your plan?'

'I'll go to college. I'll find her there. I'll make enquiries about the hostel as well.'

'Cool. Listen, if you don't find Sonal or something immediate doesn't work out, just chill and don't worry about staying here for another couple of days. Or as long as it takes. I've had friends staying over before, it's not a problem with me.'

'No, I've bothered you enough, really, I'll figure something out.'

'Look, if you find Sonal and you're going to stay with her, that's cool. But if you don't and you need a short-term option till you figure out a regular place to stay, just come and stay here. Really, it's not a bother for me at all, I, er, like the company.'

'Okay, let's see, I'll find Sonal.'

◾

She went in for her bath and came out smelling all fruity and girly. I felt vaguely embarrassed. Her hair was wet and I tried not to look at her. We moved around my small flat doing our separate things. Then she was ready to go, immaculately coiffured, fresh and angelic, while I sat there in my shorts and untidy hair and two-day stubble. 'So what time should I return by? When do you expect to get home?'

'I haven't made my plans for the day. Can you call me before you leave from wherever you are, if that's not a problem?'

'Okay. I'll call you. Thank you for everything, you're a very kind person.'

'That's a lie. I routinely push old ladies in front of cars under the pretext of helping them cross the road.'

'Bye!'

■

I called Thombre.

'Hello, Thombresaab, this is Abir Ganguly, I'm not disturbing you, am I? I hope I haven't woken you up.'

I'd realized after dialling his number that maybe this was a bit early in the day.

'No, Ganguly, it's okay. Bolo.'

'Thombresaab, that story I was going to do on you, when can I come and meet you for it?'

'You're doing story?'

'Yes, but don't worry, I'll treat the matter sensitively, I'll say only good things about you.'

How I had fallen.

'How much time you will need?'

'At least half an hour, maybe more, if that's okay.'

'Saturday fine? I will take you and feed you kombdi wada.'

'Er, actually Thombresaab, you know how it is with journalists and deadlines. I'll be very grateful if we can meet sooner. If you have some time today...'

'What you are doing now?'

'Nothing.'

'Okay, you come home now. I will go to station late, you come home.'

'Okay, how do I get there?'

I took down his address. Then I took the fastest bath ever, breaking the world record for fast baths unless we include wind-assisted times. Then I sprinted out of the house.

Thombre lived in the imaginatively named Police Quarters. The colony appeared humble from outside. I found my way to his quarter.

'Ganguly! Come in, Ganguly, come in. Welcome to humble house. No, you can keep shoes on!'

I took my shoes off anyway and walked in. The flat was small, as you'd expect a government residence for an inspector to be, but it was plush in a nouveau riche kind of way. There was a large, hideous maroon sofa set; a funky music system with Bose speakers; an ornate side table with 8413 knick-knacks crowded onto it; a lovely Kashmiri carpet that was surely hafta from some carpet shop; and a TV so large that it almost accomplished the non-Euclidean feat of being bigger than the wall behind it.

Thombre caught me looking at it and announced: 'Plasma!'

I smiled. He offered me tea.

'Uh, I don't have tea, Thombresaab. Will there be coffee...?'

'Of course, coffee.' He popped his head into the next room and shouted instructions to someone, asking for *'Deluxe* coffee.' I didn't bother specifying that I liked it black. Mustn't make too many demands. We sat.

'So tell me, what you want to know? Will picture come?'

'Picture? Oh, yes. Someone from our office will call you and come over to take photographs.'

'Good. And what you want to write about me?'

'Well, I thought I'd just write about your life, the kind of person you were before you joined the police, why you joined the police, all the things you have done, and so on.'

'That is like book then! You should write book on me! You can give it name, *In the Line of Fire!*'

'Er...'

'I am joking. I can also joke! Only you can joke kya? Ha ha ha.'

'Ha ha.'

'Tell me, what you want to know?'

I placed my recorder and notebook on the table. We began.

'See, when I was growing up, I saw the power of police.' Thombre was telling me about his childhood; his father had also been a cop. 'When I was in school, one day, my friend Santya got message that his mother was ill. I went to home with him. His mother was panting, out of breath, her neighbour were with her. They were about to take to government hospital. I also went. But at government hospital, they were ignoring. Outside, person at reception told, you sit, have water. All doctor busy. She was feeling very ill. I knew something wrong. I lost my temper, shouted at hospital person, you are hospital, aunty is ill, you should give treatment. She told me, nothing I can do. No doctor now. Till doctor come, fill up form.

'So I got frustrate. My father's police station was half kilometre. I ran to station. He got shock, he said, what you are doing, is your mother okay? I said she is fine, but Santya's mother ill, hospital ignoring her. I told him what happened. He came with me to hospital. I am telling you, whole tune of hospital changed. Santya's mother got treatment. They treated like VIP.'

'What was wrong with the lady? She was getting a heart attack or something?'

'I don't remember. But see Ganguly, this is just one example. All through childhood, I saw power of police. See, my father policeman, we were lucky. Rest family all other job – one uncle mechanic, one uncle peon, all family poor. And poor people in poor country, no one cares, no one gives bhav. Everything is power system. If you have power, people care. If you have power, you can do things. What power does poor person have?'

'Well, in theory, the power of his vote.'

'You are right, theory. But you see practical! What difference vote makes? You are voting for MP, MLA, they are far away. You see only during election. If your electricity connection gone for days, who will listen to you? If road outside your quarter dug up, or garbage pile, who will listen to you? MP, MLA, far away. Everything is power.'

'So you joined the police because of the power equations?'

'See, that is simple way of putting it. But you think of me then. You are in my position, young man, want to get married, have family, what life you will give them? Police people getting respect. Police people getting things done. Also, I saw my father: he help so many people because he was police. It was life of respect.

'And Ganguly, in my time, India not like today. I was simple graduate. No career option. These days you have IT, call centre, all modern thing. All children go abroad, even my son want to go abroad, study, do MBA. He listen to iPod. In my time, for person like me, nothing was there. I was not intellectual quality to do UPSC and join civil service at centre. But MPSC I could do. So I gave exam, pass, and I was in police. My family was so happy. All my friend look at me with full respect. Earlier, they respect me because I was police officer son. Now, I was police officer myself!'

◢

'Yes, it is hard life,' Thombre agreed. 'See, you reporter people, you see constable, havaldar on road with paunch and danda, you think, what he will protect me, he is so unfit. But why does he have belly? He has belly because his lifestyle unhealthy. He work harder than your MBA or IT person. He on road all day, or station all day, following case, dealing with criminal. He get little holiday. He get little free time. He can't take children to movie – no time. He can't take wife to restaurant – no time. He can't exercise – no time. So he get belly. But I tell you something, Ganguly – he still tough. He can still fight criminal. It hard job, but he has sense of duty. He is police!'

I didn't have it in my heart to mention the headline I'd seen in that day's *Afternoon Mail*: 'Nigerian Beats Up Three Havaldars'. Apparently three havaldars went to a brothel, found some random Nigerian dude there, and tried to arrest him. The dude thrashed the three constables. All of them ended up in hospital. One of them had a broken leg. The *Mail* had a photograph that showed his leg, all strung up, in the foreground, with the constable lying on a bed behind it. The caption read: 'Who will protect the protectors?'

My coffee arrived. As his servant placed it on the table, Thombre got up, yelled 'SHARDA!' in the general direction of the plasma TV, and disappeared into the next room. The servant left. I took a sip of the coffee.

Immediately, I imagined the following scene: Thombre in the kitchen yells, 'SHARDA, SHARDA!' A cow enters. 'Ah, Sharda, here you are,' says Thombre. He gestures to his servant, who places my coffee, still a pristine black, below Sharda. Sharda wiggles and positions her teats above my cup. The servant bends and starts milking Sharda. My coffee turns whiter and whiter, till it's basically milk, the coffee powder as diluted as homeopathic medicine. After half an hour of milking, Sharda collapses from exhaustion. The servant whips away my cup of the-beverage-formerly-known-as-coffee and puts it on a table nearby. Then he lifts his bucket of sugar.

'How is your coffee? I hope everything all right?' Thombre was back.

'Yes, Thombresaab, just perfect.'

'Good, good. I was asking my wife if any prasad from Shirdi was left. We went to Shirdi last week.'

'Oh, please don't bother...'

'No bother, Ganguly! You are guest! Have some prasad. Prasad is coming.'

The servant now returned with prasad. I refrained from saying 'Hello, Prasad' to him. I took the obligatory mouthful, chewed messily, and as I swallowed it, a young girl ran into the room saying, 'Daddy, Daddy!' She saw me, realized Daddy had a visitor, and blushed.

'Ah, Manisha. Ganguly, my daughter Manisha. Manisha, do namaste to uncle.'

'Namaste!'

'Namaste,' I said, possibly more embarrassed than Manisha.

'What is it, Manisha?' Thombre asked her in Marathi. 'Anything important?'

'Daddy, painting!' She clutched a painting in her hand, but held it by her side, shy now that I was also there.

'Another painting! Wah beta, you will make MF Husain retire like this. Show, show.'

She showed him the painting. 'Hmm, very good,' said Thombre. 'Now show to Ganguly uncle also.'

Smiling and blushing, she held out the painting. 'Very nice,' I said. 'What is it?'

'It is a boat,' she said.

It looked like a duck to me. 'Wow, that's fantastic,' I said. 'Your daddy may be a police officer, but you are an artist!'

'I can also be policeman,' she said. 'I will be policeman artist. I will draw sketch of criminal.'

And their getaway ducks, I thought.

Her father laughed indulgently, and told her to go inside and play, Daddy is discussing important things. She went.

'She wants to be a policeman?'

'Oh, no, she will never do what I do. She want to be different thing every five minutes. If I tell her you are journalist, she will say, "Daddy, I want to be journalist." She want to be everything!'

'You have any other kids?'

'Yes, one son, Rushabh, he is not at home now, gone to college. Rushabh in junior college, studying science. He is very smart, very ambitious. No one would think I am his baap, he is so smart! He will go abroad and study, he say, do MBA. I told, you go to best college, don't worry about fee, I will pay fee. He said, Daddy, I will not take one paisa from you.

I will get scholarship! I will do it on my own! I felt so proud, Ganguly. My children make me proud.

'And my daughter also, she very smart. She so good at math, much better than her mother or me. She read book, big book, so fat, it could be murder weapon! Only book I read when I was young was guidebook for entrance exam. She also want to go abroad.'

'And you're happy with that?'

'Arre, of course! I want her go, be independent. You know, I am tradition man, but I don't believe in getting daughter married early. She should make own identity, she should stand on feet. She should never dependent on man. Ganguly, in my day, we had no option. Even if we did, I was not smart enough, ha ha ha. But my children, they will do much better than me.'

■

I had asked Thombre for half an hour of his time, but I ended up sitting with him for almost two. I asked him all the questions I'd written down in my notebook, and got some great answers. He was full of anecdotes of things that policemen did; he helped me understand the career path of a typical policeman; his ambitions, what motivates him, what frustrates him; what the day in the life of a police inspector in Bombay looks like.

And afterwards, as he showed me out, we spoke for another 15 minutes off the record.

'Ganguly, you ask me earlier, how I deal with underworld, underworld have political contacts. Hmm? Your tape recorder on, I give standard answer, politician don't interfere, policeman do duty, phalana dhimkana. Now your tape recorder off, I give you real answer. This whole world, this whole world you see around you: it is all underworld.

'I told you earlier, everything is power system. The government, it is like don. Don take hafta, government take tax. Don have gunda, government have police. Only difference, don have competition, government have no competition, government have monopoly. Only at election time, different gang fight to take control of government monopoly. It is best business.

'Gunda take hafta, all government servant take bribe. Why they take bribe? Because they have power over common man. Government not servant of people, government ruler of people. Government most powerful mafia.

'To get posting to some police stations, policemen have to pay lakhs, even more than crore. Policeman earn few thousand a month. Why he pay so much? Because some station, more money than others. Because like corner shop, even for mafia, location matter.

'Other mafia also try to operate. Every gang look around, where is money to be made? Builder have black money, call builder, ask protection money. Government don't allow prostitution, open brothel, give people what they want if government won't allow. Competition, Ganguly. That is why government has to keep law and order. To kill the competition.

'And sometime, like company do deal, like company make strategic partnership, government also make deal with underworld. You operate here, give me hafta. Some underworld group pay off politician. They do dirty work, politician also make money, win-win. So underworld group tie up with politician – and underworld gang tie up with police also.

'Within police, Ganguly, there are two kind encounter policeman: Rajan police and Dawood police. Rajan police kill only Dawood man. Dawood police kill only Rajan man. It is not about law and order. It is competition. It is business.'

'Wow,' I said. 'So, er, where do you come in all this?'

'I am law-abiding, dutiful police officer,' he said. 'But I will tell something. In so many years of fighting underworld, so many encounter, I have only killed Musalman.'

A chill went up my spine. In the distance I could hear the sound of his daughter laughing. Someone revved up a motorcycle behind me. Then I realized I wasn't breathing, and inhaled.

'All this off the record, Ganguly. Because you are friend, and you should know real world.'

'Thank you, Thombresaab,' I said. 'There's just one small thing I'm curious about, completely off the record. That Muslim chap you killed that night, that Iqbal fellow, are you really sure he was a gangster?'

Thombre sighed. 'Ganguly, that evening I got tipoff that gangster would be at that address. Two or three gangster, sleeping. Not dangerous gangster, just courier people for Chhota Sion, people who carry drugs from here to there. I was told it was house of accountant of that gang, and three-four other men were with him, with drug. I did not expect action, firing. If I did, I would not call you there. I am not fool, to put you in danger. I thought, simple arrest, maybe we find drug, we display powder, have men in hathkadi, good story for you, progress for us.

'My informer, he was never wrong before. He risk life every time he give us information. Anyway, there was misunderstanding, the man there got angry, one of my man lost control, and it happened. Was he gangster now? I don't know. My informer say he was sure, he got his information from good place. He never let me down before. He gave me good information after. We act in good faith only.

'But sometime, people make mistake. Everybody make mistake, it is not like only police make mistake.'

'Hmm, okay.'

'Don't worry, Ganguly, Bombay is big city. City move on, people move on. Life move on.'

'Yes. Thank you for talking to me, Thombresaab, I'm very grateful.'

'It is my pleasure. Tell me when photographer come to take picture. And you also fix time and come to station. I will take you to kombdi wada. You are my favourite reporter, hardworking boy.'

'Thank you, sir, I'll definitely be in touch. Bye.'

I walked over to a nearby dosa joint and ordered an uthappa. It was lunchtime. I asked for extra chutney and dug in. I felt lucky that I was who I was.

Yes, yes, self-loathing is fashionable and I cultivate it well. But really, had I been born in Thombre's place, with his background, his parents, his circumstances, I have no doubt that I'd have turned out worse. Yes, *worse*: I would have been the lazy schmuck who failed to clear his MPSC and ended up as a mechanic somewhere, or maybe tried for a lower grade of government job, and was miserable – genuinely miserable, not just down because angst is fashionable. I'd have looked at a career path like Thombre's with envy. He had made the best of what life had thrown his way. I couldn't bring myself to condemn him on moral grounds – the world around him, *the real world* as he put it, had no place for morality. He did what he had to.

I should have hated him because he killed Muneeza's dad. I never knew Mohammad Iqbal, but when I looked at Muneeza, the state she was in, fragile but trying to keep it together, wanting to cry but not having a shoulder to cry on, his death felt like a personal tragedy. I could have killed that man who killed Mohammad Iqbal – but on the other side of that coin, I understood that man, even admired him slightly.

Well, at least I had a story. I was looking forward to writing the half of the feature that was about Thombre's life.

Or was I?

11. A Walk on the Beach

I went home intending to instantly start transcribing Thombre's tape, and sat down on the divan with the best of intentions. Ten minutes later I was asleep. In my hostel days I was known as a ferocious napper, and my friends used to tease me that my Bengali genes made me nap. Even Robida napped, I would tell them, even Manikda napped. All great artists napped.

And what is your art, they would ask.

Napping, I would reply.

◼

I had a dream that I was an Eskimo, and Thombre visited me in my igloo. 'I have come to arrest you,' he said.

'Please don't arrest me.'

'No, I will arrest.'

'But why? What will you get if you arrest me?'

'Aha! Wrong question! Right question, what I will get if I *don't* arrest?'

'Thombresaab, I'm just a poor journalist. I have no money.'

'Scotch?'

'Scotch?'

'You have Scotch?'

'Er, yes.'

'Give Scotch.'

I went to the cabinet, took out a bottle of Scotch and asked him how he'd like it. 'On the rocks,' he said.

'Er, I don't have ice,' I replied.

'Look around you,' he said. 'Do you need wall?'

Just then, the phone rang.

◾

It was Muneeza. 'Hi, Abir, this is Muneeza. Are you at home? Can I come now?'

'Yes, of course. Is everything all right?'

'I'll be there in half an hour. Thanks.'

She hung up. I went back to sleep and tried to re-enter the dream with Thombre. I wanted to know what happened next. Where would I get the ice from?

But I was too awake to lapse back into that dream. And yet another mystery remained unsolved.

◾

I woke up to the buzzing of a mosquito, with the vague sense that something else had woken me up. What could it be? Then the doorbell rang.

It was Muneeza. I said: 'Hi! I'm sorry, have you been ringing the bell for long? I was asleep.'

'Sorry, I didn't mean to wake you up.'

'Don't be silly, it's only, what, eight o'clock. This is no time to be sleeping. Thank goodness you woke me up. How was your day? Is everything okay?'

At this point she started to cry. We were standing at the door, which was still ajar. I shut it, and asked her what happened as she rushed towards the bathroom, muttering 'sorry'. I waited outside. She came back. She'd washed her face; her eyes were red.

'Muneeza, what happened?'

'I went to college, and I went looking for Sonal, and her friend from Thane told me that she has gone out of town with her family, she doesn't know when they are returning, she thinks maybe next week.'

'Cool, so that's hardly a problem, you can stay here till then.'

'Then I made enquiries about the hostel. They said there's no vacancy now, but there will be when the new semester starts, I should apply then.'

'Muneeza, Muneeza... so what's the problem? You're not on the street, you can stay here, there's no need to be upset.'

'I'm not upset about that.'

'Oh.'

'Abir, you're very kind, but I can't stay here like this, it's too much. I have to manage on my own. So I went home before coming here, I thought I'll somehow stay there. After all, it was my home for so many years.'

'And?'

'And... I couldn't.' She looked into my eyes for the first time that evening, and I thought she would cry again. 'I should be strong,' she said. 'Abbu would have expected me to be strong. But I'm *not* strong! I *can't* do this!'

She looked down again. I touched her arm.

'Muneeza, dude, I understand. But don't make it worse for yourself by making the situation out to be worse than it is. Please don't worry about not having a place to stay. You stay here till Sonal comes back, you stay here till your next semester starts, you stay here till whenever. I also stayed with a friend for free when I first came to Bombay. That's what friends are for. It's not a big deal. You can trust me.'

'I know I can trust you,' she said. 'It's not about that. But it's too much to ask, too much. I've just known you for a few days.'

'Well, I feel like we're old friends already. Maybe new old friends, but you know what I mean. If this was a bother for me, I wouldn't ask. But it really isn't, and I like your company, even if it makes me a little nervous.'

'Why nervous?'

'Well, you know, you're a girl, and I have to make sure I don't use any bad words, and, um, I'm joking! It's fine. You can't just randomly wake me up and expect me to be articulate. Come, what do you want to do for dinner? Would you like to order or shall we go out somewhere?'

'Abir... I'll stay here till Sonal comes, and I'll never forget this favour. I'll always...'

'It's not a favour. Don't get all melodramatic now, or shehnai will start playing in my head, and I totally hate that.'

She smiled. I patted her head, fighting the urge to run my hand through her hair, and said something silly like *don't worry*. She said she'd just freshen up and come. She left the room, and I sat there with a hard-on. So here this girl was upset because her father had died and she felt alone and helpless, and I was erect. Physical proximity and all is okay, but I had no business being horny at this time. I looked down and said to my organ:

'This is not the time. Behave yourself!'

It replied: 'I'm behaving myself only. No confusion there. You're the dude who seems unclear about what's going on. I wonder sometimes, are you the dick or am I?'

◾

I took Muneeza to Rajma Singh Da Dhaba for dinner, and we sat on a khatiya and ate food. Who had ever thought khatiyas would become a fashion statement, and we yuppie folk would be sitting on a surface of criss-crossing rope, feeling all hip and cool while our bums hurt? Anyway, so there we sat and ordered rajma and alu mattar and saag paneer and many rotis, and spoke about me because, obviously, we couldn't speak about her.

'No, really, I was horribly immature in those days, a complete wannabe buffoon.' I was telling her about a play I'd written in college with three characters in it: the Id, the Ego and the Superego. Thank God everyone refused to act in it, or it might be on YouTube today and people would still be making fun of me.

'All these new technologies,' I continued, 'I love them, but the problem they present is this: they record everything. So you're an enthu college dude and you upload all your bad poems on your blogspot blog and do silly things on YouTube and so on, and five years later you think, what a bloody immature brat I was! But it's too late, it's all out there, the whole world knows — now you're an immature brat for posterity, even when you're 65 and have grandchildren who've grown past that phase.'

'But you can delete all that.'

'Yes, yes, of course, but traces always remain. You can run but you can't hide.'

'But how do you know you're not immature now? Ten years later you might look back on the person you are now and find him immature and boyish also.'

'Why, you find me immature and boyish?'

'No, of course not. You're very responsible. Achha, tell me about your family.'

'Mmm, not much to speak of. I'm an only child. My father died a few years ago, as you know. My mother is a corporate honcho in Calcutta. She's a totally formidable woman. I believe her department in the company where she works is known as the Amazon because of her. And, um, that's it.'

'Do you miss your mother? Did you consider taking a job in Calcutta?'

'Oh no, no way. I would never do that. I mean, I like my mom and all, but in small doses. I couldn't bear to actually live with her. Also, I like Bombay. The traffic is terrible, but once you get used to it, and you have your own little hangouts, it's hard to leave. This city gives you a rush. When I go away on holiday now, I even feel nostalgic about the local trains, that's how much of a Bombay junkie I've become. And also, even though we have the dirtiest beaches in the world, I enjoy sitting by the sea. Hey, you wanna go to Juhu beach after this?'

◼

We walked for a bit on the beach, deftly avoiding the garbage around us, ignoring the ragged urchins playing ball and the vendors casting lewd looks.

'The trick is to lose yourself in the breeze and look out towards the sea. Focus on the far, not the near.'

'You sound like a meditation teacher.'

'Eh? Sorry! No, I'm very embarrassed about this beach, so whenever I've come here with someone out of town, I need to tell them to focus on the things that really matter.'

'Now you sound like a new age author. Also, I'm not from outside town, even if you just met me recently.'

'Sorry, I didn't mean it that way! It's just that I've met you recently, so you seem like someone not from my world, so I keep introducing my world to you.'

'Bombay's sea could also be in my world.'

'Yes, but while your sea and my sea are the same sea, they're also totally different seas. If you get what I mean.'

'Yes. So we're on different beaches now, talking across beaches?'

'Okay, fine, I'll stop being postmodern. Hey, look!'

'What?'

'Turd!'

'So have you always wanted to be a journalist?'

'No, not really.'

'So what did you want to be?'

'Well, nothing in particular. I mean, at any point in my life if you asked me what I wanted to do, I'd have an answer. When I was five, I'd say I wanted to be a pilot. When I was 10, I'd say I wanted to be a rock musician – and all my uncles and aunties would irritate the hell out of me saying *oooh, how cuuute!* When I was 15, I told everyone I wanted to be an entrepreneur, to do an MBA and all that. Then, when I graduated, I told people I wanted to be a journalist, because I enjoyed writing. And because I told people that I wanted to be this, or I wanted to be that, I believed it myself. I became ambitious because it was expected of me.'

'But what do you want to be now? Where would you like to be 10 years from now?'

'Hmm, I don't know. See, I find journalism boring and pointless. But it's not that there is something else that I'm passionate about. I just want to live comfortably, eat good food, buy all the books and music that I want, see the latest flicks so I can make fun of them. I don't feel like I have a calling and a vocation. But you know, that doesn't mean that if I was a rich dude's son, and could do all these things and not have to work, I would be happy. There would still be an empty space around what I wanted to do with my life. I haven't filled it yet. What about you, Muneeza?'

She sighed. 'I feel the same way, Abir. I don't know what I want to be. I mean, some of my friends, they would be happy to get married and have children and so on. But I don't see the point of that. I mean, I would like that sometime, I'm sure it will happen, but that's not the main aim of my life. I guess I'm like you, I don't know what I want to do. Except that you're much smarter than me.'

'Are you crazy? Don't be ridiculous. If I was smart I wouldn't be a journalist.'

'No, but you have to be smart to be a journalist, no? All these pieces you write.'

'Clearly you haven't being paying attention to what newspapers carry these days. It's all junk. There's no value. I'm just a hack.'

'No, you're not. I mean, I don't know, maybe you are! But you're much smarter than most people I know. You shouldn't be so hard on yourself.'

'If you insist. Shall we turn back now?'

'Yes, I'm tired also. Today was a very tiring day.'

As we walked back, after a minute or so, she asked: 'Abir, you don't have a girlfriend?'

'No.'

'How come?'

'I'm gay.'

'Shut up.'

'Like that only, yaar. Who will go out with someone like me?'

Deep inside, for some reason, I was punching the air.

12. A Content, Demented Baby

I tend to sleep all curled up with a pillow, as if it is a lover I'm holding tenderly — or, if I had a bad dream, a panda I grabbed and crushed in my sleep. I didn't have a bad dream that night, and in the morning I must have looked ridiculous, embracing my pillow, smiling like a content, demented baby. That's when Muneeza woke me up.

'Abir,' she whispered loudly when I opened my eyes. 'Sorry for waking you up. I'm going to college. I'll be done by lunch. Will you be at home?'

'Eh, ah, ooh. Ya, I'll be here.'

'Should I call before coming?'

'No, I'll be here.'

'Thanks, bye!'

'Stop whispering. I'll go deaf.'

She smiled, got up and walked off elegantly. I hugged the pillow.

'Consider yourself lucky,' the pillow said. 'I could have been a panda.'

◾

I finally got up at about 11, stumbled to the computer, checked my email. None of my regular correspondents had let me down. There were emails offering me Viagra. There was an email telling me I had won the Grand Lotto. (Again!) There was the usual query asking me if I wanted a larger penis, despite the fact that I had sent them pictures of my mammoth 12-inch organ to get them to stop. And there was Mrs Grace writing from Nigeria – just the kind of sweet old lady you want to run over with a truck.

I checked out India Uncut and all the regular sites I visit, but on autopilot more than out of genuine interest. Then I logged out. I needed to work.

I don't fully wake up until an hour after getting up from bed, and copious amounts of coffee are required. I drank one cup at home; then I decided to go out and have another cup at the nearby CCD. Also, I needed to get a duplicate key for the house made, so that Muneeza would not be dependent on my being home.

I went to the bathroom to brush my teeth. As I shut the door, I saw that Muneeza, probably in a hurry that morning, had left a bra hanging on the hook behind the door. The bra and I eyed each other warily for a couple of seconds. Then I gave up and left the bathroom, shutting the door behind me as if a venomous snake lay behind it.

'You fool, even you have a snake,' said a voice from below my belt.

'Shut up,' I replied. 'I'm a virtuous, well brought-up, middle-class boy. And besides, I really like this girl.'

■

I got the duplicate key made, and then I sat at CCD for half an hour with my notebook, forwarding through my tapes of Thombre speaking, making notes about the things I wanted to include in my piece, figuring out its structure. While I always use my dictaphone for interviews, I never rely on it. I also make my own notes, both mental and on paper, while interviewing someone. If I'm paying attention, I find that I hardly need the recorded audio later. Most of the people I speak to don't speak perfect English, or often *any* English, and my job becomes not to get their exact words down but to capture the gist of what they're saying as accurately as I can. If I'm alert through the interview, I find that I remember most of it. As an old boss of mine once told me, 'What you don't remember is probably not worth recording anyway.'

Writing about Thombre, I found, was much easier than writing about Iqbal had been. In a few minutes, I had my structure down pat, and a few sentences here and there as they occurred to me. I was confident I could finish at least a draft of the entire piece today. I decided that I would go home, wait for Muneeza, have lunch with her, and then go to office and finish the draft there. Then I would come back in the evening and chill with Muneeza.

I wished I didn't have the story to write. Then I could have chilled with her all day.

■

Muneeza came home, I gave her the key, we went out for a quick lunch at a nearby udipi.

'I'm amazed you eat outside food all the time. You'll spoil your stomach like this.'

'I know, I have an aunt who keeps asking me when I'm getting married so I can have someone cook for me. I told her that I've put my profile on shaadi.com. She was upset, she said she could find me better girls, why go through a website, family connections make all the difference.'

'You've put your profile on shaadi.com?'

'Of course not. I just told my aunt that. I love pulling her leg, such as it is. I call her my roly-poly stereophonic aunty. She's a big ball of exuberant Bonghood. Lovely lady.'

'Uh... okay. Where does she live?'

'She's in Delhi these days. Her husband is the MD of a company that manufactures hydraulic motors or something. I suspect everyone in my family would be very happy if I also did something like that. Can you imagine? Hydraulic motors?'

'No, you are definitely made for better things. Have you ever considered pneumatic pumps?'

'Heh. That's just the kind of thing I would say. I think we're made for each other.'

And suddenly, with that joke, the conversation stopped. We were both embarrassed. I called the waiter and asked for extra chutney. I didn't actually eat any of it, though. Horrible chutney.

◆

I bumped into Sandhya and Mahesh as I got into the lift. They seemed to be coming from lunch somewhere — no doubt having spent as much on it as my monthly salary.

'Oh, Abir, hi,' said Sandhya. 'I was just going to go up and call you. How's the story coming along? We need it soon, we're making dummy copies of the paper, and I'd like to be able to run an actual story on it.'

'It's going well. I know I should have given it today, but I'm hoping to finish a draft by tomorrow sometime? Is that okay?'

'Hmm, tomorrow what time?'

'By evening,' I said, playing it safe. 'Maybe late evening.'

'Well, actually anyway I'm out of town tomorrow and back on Monday. Just finish it before the weekend's over, please, so I can read it first thing Monday morning.'

'I'll email it to you then?'

'No, don't do that, I like reading on paper, I'm old-fashioned that way.' Sandhya and Mahesh smiled at one another. 'Why don't you take a printout and leave it in my cabin? Just put it on my computer keyboard. When I get in to work, I'll just pick it up from there.'

'Okay, will do.'

'And how's it going?'

'Er, good. I'm trying my best to make it work. When does the paper come out?'

'Well, it's probably delayed now, we'll take some time to launch it. But we need dummy copies so we can show it to the trade, and maybe to investors. That's what I need the story for.'

The lift reached our floor, and we got off. I headed to my computer and buckled down to work.

▪▪

'And what are you listening to so intently, young man?' asked D'Souza, eyeing my headphones warily. 'Eminem?'

'Oh, hello, sir. No, I don't listen to Eminem. I'm transcribing an interview.'

'An interview! Transcribing! The boy works, does he? I wish you had been this industrious when you worked in my department.'

'I was, sir. I worked very hard. You want to see my highest score in Tetris?'

D'Souza looked at me disbelievingly, and then smiled. I smiled back. Hey, we were joking around. At this rate we'd be a couple soon.

▪▪

I wrote till evening, and got through about 3000 words on Thombre. Since Thombre constituted about half my piece, I'd have to cut this by half. So which bits would I cut? How would I intersperse this narrative with what I'd written about Muneeza's dad? These were knotty problems best tackled with a fresh mind. I was tired, and looking forward to going home.

◼

I rang the bell to give warning of my arrival, then used the key to enter. Muneeza was on her way to open the door, holding a knife, tears in her eyes.

Then she smiled and wiped the sweat off her forehead. 'Onions,' she said. 'I was cutting onions.'

I followed her into the kitchen. There were onions. There were potatoes. There were green things that dedicated carnivores like me try not to acknowledge. It was like a parallel universe.

'I'm sorry,' she said. 'I should have asked you. But I just thought, you eat out every day, let me cook something for us at home. So I went out and got some vegetables. I hope you don't mind.'

'No,' I said, wondering if it was prudent to read some deeper significance into this. But nah, you stay with a friend, you help out at home, this was par for the course. I shouldn't read too much into it.

'Um, this is very sweet of you, but you needn't have bothered, really.'

'It's not a bother, you'll like what I make, promise.'

'I'm sure I will. Let me help you then. Is there something I can do?'

'No, don't worry, it's all under control. Can you cook?'

'When I was a child, I won the toast-making competition in my building. Of course, I cheated – I used an automatic toaster.'

'Hmm.'

'And in college, I was a Maggi-making legend.'

'Your sense of humour is horrible.'

'Thanks, I have that effect on women sometimes. They tell me my sense of humour is horrible – and then they cook for me.'

'I'm beginning to think twice about cooking, now.'

'Come, let's go out then. It's been a long time since I had Lebanese food.'

'Sit!'

'Lebanese...'

'Sit! You can eat Indian today.'

'Okay. Fine. Bully me.'

A couple of seconds passed and then I moved out of the kitchen – or we'd have spent the night smiling goofily at each other, and maybe even sung a song around a tree or something.

◼

I should mention here that dinner was good. And when it was done, I made coffee. That was good too.

It was overall a fine evening: we ate and drank and bantered about this, and bantered about that, and bantered about banter. Then we said good night and I didn't lean forward and take her in my arms and kiss her on the lips, we just said good night and she went into the room. And I lay back on my divan and thought of how happy I was. I thought, like a silly boy: *This was the best evening of my life.*

Then I remembered my deadline, and how much of my piece I still needed to write. I'm telling you, I wanted to die right then.

Had I done so, I might well have bumped into Mohammad Iqbal in heaven.

'That's my daughter you were flirting with.'

'I know. Er, sir... hello!'

'Hello, my ass. You were thinking of hugging and kissing my daughter.'

'How do you know that?'

'I could read your mind. We dead people can read the mind of everyone who's alive.'

'Oops.'

'We can see you naked in the bath as well. I can't tell you how much fun I've had since I died – my former neighbour Mrs Golwalkar is more of a hottie than I imagined. But leave that aside. I am very upset with you because you were having nude, I mean, lewd thoughts about my daughter.'

'But I haven't done anything untoward, have I?'

'That's because you have died. Otherwise who knows what you would have gotten up to?'

'Who?'

'Who what?'

'Who knows what I would have gotten up to?'

He slapped his head, and because he was a spectral presence, his hand went right through the back of his head. He looked quite funny, but then he corrected himself, put his arm back in place and said: 'You're ridiculous, you make me want to die again. Thank goodness my daughter is spared of you. Or who knows what would happen?'

'Who?'

13. Mannequin and Ma

Some people wake up fresh, ready to conquer the world. Others wake up ready to go back to sleep. I'm in the second category, but when I woke up that morning I felt like a conqueror. I heard Muneeza messing about in the kitchen. 'World, here I come!' That was fair warning, and I went striding into the kitchen.

'Oh, hi, Abir. Sorry, did I wake you up by moving around here? I was trying to be quiet.'

'No, no, of course not, I woke up by myself. What's up, off to college?'

'Yes. I have a lot of catching up to do before the exams. Can I make you some coffee?'

'No, dude, chill, I'll make it for myself later. So what does your day look like?'

'I'll be in college all morning, back late in the afternoon. What about you?'

'I need to work on my piece in the morning.

Once I'm fully awake, I'll see whether I want to do it here or go to office.'

'Okay. See you later then.'

'Take care.'

'Oh, Abir, just one thing, I've been thinking...'

'Hmm.'

'It's not fair that I should displace you from your bedroom while you sleep in the hall. From tonight you please shift back to your bedroom. I can sleep in the hall.'

'I prefer the hall. I can work late into the night that way.'

'Oh, you can work as late as you want even if I'm sleeping in the hall, the light doesn't bother me. Even Abbu often kept the light on. But it's not fair that you should sacrifice your bedroom for me.'

'Muneeza, you worry too much. Between the hall and the bedroom, I actually prefer the hall. It's a great hall. It's better than the Royal Albert Hall. It's...'

'You're very difficult! I'm going to resume this argument when I return. You're being too much of a good host.'

'I am a good Bengali boy. And one day I will be a good Bengali man. Do you know what a good Bengali needs to become a man from a boy?'

'A wife?'

'No. A paunch.'

I went to office late in the morning. I worked for a couple of hours. That is to say, I tried to work. My mind kept wandering, and the internet gave it places to wander to. Every three minutes I told myself, *Just two minutes more, let me just check out this page, then I will work.* But I'd check out that page, and click on a link there, or think of something because of what I was reading and go somewhere else, and so on and on until it was almost lunchtime and I was better informed about the world but less so about my own piece.

When this happens, I ward off guilt by telling myself that I'm incubating. My subconscious whirs, I rationalize – though if my subconscious is anything like the rest of me, it probably naps.

I went off to lunch at Eterniti. I bought a magazine from Bookends and sat in the food court, nursing a tuna sandwich and then a black coffee. I felt suddenly low now – not because I hadn't got any work done, but because I couldn't see what lay ahead of me. I felt pre-emptively nostalgic for my current happiness, which would surely end. I was happy being with Muneeza at the moment – but I was putting off two inevitable confrontations. One, I needed to confront myself about what this all meant, and how seriously I took it. Two, I needed to talk to her, to be completely honest about all the things she did not know.

But what did that mean anyway? And what were the ramifications? This was all too complicated for me at the moment, so I turned my attention back to the strangers around me, playing my old game of speculating about their lives.

◼

As I finished lunch, my phone rang. It was Ganesh, an old college friend of mine, now also in Bombay, inviting me to a party at his place that evening.

'I've moved into a new flat in Juhu,' he said. 'This is a housewarming party – and you know how my parties are! Much alcohol, hot chicas.'

'I'll see, I'm not sure, I have a bit of work I'm trying to finish off.'

'Hey, don't be silly, you'll enjoy yourself, we won't get you *too* sloshed. Some old college pals will be there, Sameer and Neha, Ash, Puneet, Baldy, Cyrus, many of my co-workers at Lintas, such as the very hot Ramona, whom you've met. Come, dude, you'll enjoy yourself, I'll SMS my address once I finish calling everyone, 8pm sharp.'

'Okay, let me see how things are in the evening.'

'Great. And listen, feel free to bring a friend along if you want. See ya!'

After lunch I ambled around inside the mall, window-shopping. *I really like Bombay's weather,* I often tell friends from out of town, *especially in the air-conditioned malls.*

While passing 2 Kewl, the clothes store, I was attacked. A female mannequin wearing just a black t-shirt jumped off the window display and rushed towards me. I turned and tried to escape, but it leapt on me and pinned me to the ground. 'Don't kill me, please don't kill me,' I begged. 'I have a deadline to meet. I have responsibilities. I have a friend who needs me.'

'Oh, I will certainly kill you,' said the mannequin, 'unless you buy the t-shirt I'm wearing.'

'Excuse me,' I said, remembering to be polite even in this time of great stress. 'That's a t-shirt for girls.'

'You fool, I'm not asking you to buy it for yourself. Buy it for your friend, Sancho.'

'How do you know about, er, Sancho?'

'I saw her looking at the t-shirt the other day at the mall, when she was walking by with you. The look in her eyes told me she thought it was smart. I think you should buy it for her.'

'What about you? What will you wear?'

'You fool, I'm a mannequin.'

■

I entered the store and asked the store attendant for that shirt. He asked me what size I wanted. 'Er, I'm not sure,' I said.

Just then my eyes fell on a girl in the store who was browsing through a rack of t-shirts with (presumably) her boyfriend. She looked Muneeza's size. I wondered if I should ask her what her size was when she and her boyfriend both looked at me, and I realized that I'd been staring at her breasts.

As I looked up at their faces in alarm and embarrassment, I also realized that I'd run into these two earlier. This was the couple who had been making out in the seats behind Muneeza and me in the theatre.

'You, I know you,' barked the guy. 'You are same boy who was staring at my girlfriend in cinema hall. You are pervert.'

'No, no, you misunderstand. I was just about to buy a t-shirt for my friend, and I didn't know her size, and your friend is her size, so I was looking at her and wondering what size she is. I mean, t-shirt size.'

Both of them stared at me blankly. Then the guy said to the girl: 'Come, Vyajanthimala, let us go. We will be late for movie.'

They glared at me and walked out of the store. At least they could have told me her size.

'For me? Oh, you needn't have.'

'I wanted to. I thought it would look nice on you. I hope you like it.'

'Of course, but Abir, I don't know if I can accept this. This is too much...'

She was wondering about the propriety of it, as I thought she would.

'Please take it, Muneeza. I'll be hurt if you don't. And please don't read anything into it, I'm always buying gifts for my friends.'

'Okay. But you're being too kind to me.'

'Don't be ridiculous. Achha, one of my old college friends has called me to a housewarming party at his place this evening. You want to come along?'

'But I don't know any of your friends.'

'That's cool, most of the people there will only know a handful of the others. Ganesh calls all kinds of people to his parties, and most of them will be strangers to me as well. He asked me to bring a friend along if I wanted, and I thought it would be nice if you came along.'

'Abir, I'll feel awkward. You go ahead, I'll just rest here, if that's okay.'

'No, come! If you don't, I won't feel like going either. Please?'

'Okay, if you insist. What time do we go there?'

'The party starts at eight, I'm told, so we can get there by nine-ish. I'll just hop down to the laundry and see if my clothes are ready – I'm out of decent shirts to wear. You have anything you'd like me to give for washing?'

'No. I have some clothes that need washing, but I'd rather wash them myself, I'll do it tomorrow.'

'Okay.'

I ran down to the laundry, across the road. My clothes were washed but not yet ironed. I give a week's worth at a time, so it was quite a bit. I told the man at the laundry that I needed them in a hurry, and he said that he'd iron them within an hour and call me when they were ready. He took down my mobile number. I went back up and made coffee for me and Muneeza as I told her the story of how I bought the t-shirt.

'Vyajanthimala?'

'I swear I'm not making that up. Vyajanthimala!'

And we laughed and laughed and laughed, not because it was all that funny, but because laughing made it okay to show happiness.

I was in the bathroom when my phone, which I'd left in the hall, started ringing. It must be the laundry, I thought. I popped my head out and asked Muneeza if she could take the call please. Then I got back to soaping myself.

Muneeza knocked on the door.

'Ya?'

'That was your mother.'

'Oh.'

'I told her you were bathing. She's asked you to call back once you're done.'

Shit.

◖

The laundry man also called to tell me that my clothes were ready, which gave me an excuse to go downstairs and call my mother, away from Muneeza.

'Abir, who is that girl and why were you having a bath?'

'Ma, *you* taught me to have a bath. Cleanliness, remember.'

'No, what I mean to ask is, you are at home? And having a bath? And this girl is there? At this time in the evening? Is she your girlfriend? Is she staying with you? Is she Bengali?'

'Ma, don't be paranoid. She's just a friend, she dropped in home, we're going to go out for dinner, I felt sweaty after a hard day's work, so I asked her to wait while I took a quick bath. What is there in that?'

'But is she Bengali?'

'No.'

'What is she?'

'Ma, don't be ridiculous.'

'What is her name? Tell me her name.'

'Ma, her name is... Sancho.'

'Sanju? Her name is Sanju? Short for Sanjana?'

'Ma, you're thinking too much. You need to play more sudoku. It's not Sanju, it's Sancho.'

'Sancho? What kind of name is that? Is she Indian?'

'Of course she's Indian, Ma. Would I betray our great nation by going out with a foreigner?'

'Does she work in your office? What does her father do?'

'Her parents are dead.'

'Oh.'

'Ma, just chill out. It's not what you think. Don't get ahead of yourself. Okay, tell me, how are things with you?'

'Very good, shona, very good. I called to tell you that I'm passing through Bombay on Tuesday, on my way to Amsterdam. Are you working that day? I thought I'll come and check your flat, and then I can take you out for a good dinner.'

'Er, super. That's great. I'll make sure I have no work that day, my offs are flexible at the moment.'

'That's good. My flight lands at nine in the morning, I'll be in meetings till evening, then I'll come and pick you up. I will call, of course. And that girlfriend of yours, Sanju, you can bring her also if you want.'

'Sancho. She's not my girlfriend, Ma!'

'I am your mother, shona. I can tell by the tone of your voice what is what. Goodbye now, my serial is starting.'

'Bye, Ma.'

14. The Party (And the Reality Show)

Muneeza had changed into an orange silk salwar-kameez when I re-entered the house. I gaped at her. She looked gorgeous – but we weren't going to a wedding.

'I thought I should wear something proper if it's a party.'

'It's actually a casual sort of party. You look stunning in this, but, er, this is more something one wears to a formal thingie.'

'Oh.' She looked disappointed.

'Just wear everyday stuff, you don't need to dress up too much for this. Even jeans and t-shirt will do.'

She suddenly cheered up. 'I'll wear the t-shirt you gave me?'

'Yes! Who can stop you?'

She went off to change while I quickly wore my hot-off-the-press white shirt. While everyone at the party would be dressed casually, there would be one difference between the guys and the girls: the guys would be casually casual while the girls would be elaborately and painstakingly casual. There would be lots of faux-nonchalant cleavage – indeed, Muneeza might well be the only girl at the party not showing any.

I thought of the dress that Ramona had worn at the last party I'd been to at Ganesh's. Her cleavage had almost reached her belly button – one inch lower and it would have met the hem of her skirt. (Yes, I know, that seems geometrically impossible – but a horny boy's imagination knows no bounds.) I wondered how Muneeza would have looked in that dress.

'Why are you smiling like that?'

Muneeza emerged from the room, having changed, and tilted her head to look at me.

'Like that only,' I said, also tilting my head, so that if the space between us could vanish we would be kissing.

I was certain such thoughts would never enter her head. So was I a pervert? A bad, bad boy?

'Yes,' said the lizard. 'You are a pervert. I hate you. I never thought you'd turn out like this. I thought you'll always have eyes only for me – not to mention lust.'

'Do cats eat lizards?'

'Are you kidding me? Why do you ask?'

'Well, if they did, I'd have got one.'

'Forget it. This house is already too crowded. Get that babe out of here.'

◾

'You look really nice,' I told Muneeza as we got into an auto rickshaw. What a lame thing to say. But how else could I put it? What synonyms for 'beautiful' exist that aren't clichés by now? What on earth was happening to me, getting all gooey like this?

'Thanks,' she said.

◾

'Please don't tell your friends that I'm staying with you, they might misunderstand.'

'Of course I won't, Muneeza. Also, let's not tell them how we've met and all — too complicated.'

'I agree. Listen, did you call your mother?'

'Yes. When I went down to the laundry.'

'Oh. Did she ask who I was?'

'Yes.'

'What did you tell her?'

'I told her you're my friend Sancho, and she misheard and thought I'd said Sanju.'

'Sancho?'

'Yes, you told me that was your nickname. I hope, er, you don't mind I said that. I know we've only met recently...'

'No, you can call me that if you feel like. Only my father called me that, but I don't mind if you do. If you want to.'

After a few moments she asked: 'But you've always called me Muneeza so far. Why did you tell your mother my name was Sancho?'

'Er, just like that, on the spur of the moment.'

But that wasn't the real reason. Had I told my mother that the girl who answered my phone while I was in the bathroom was called 'Muneeza', she might have been alarmed, and asked more questions. Muneeza is an obviously Muslim name. My mother is modern and broad-minded by the standards of her generation, but she can still be unpredictable. I'm not sure how she would have reacted, and it wasn't a risk I needed to take — yet.

I'm always a little stressed at parties where I don't know too many people. At gigs where everybody knows everybody else, people are relaxed and no one's worried about the impression they're making on others. At parties like the ones Ganesh likes to host, though, most people are strangers, and they're all young, and hormones float through the air like perfume. Everyone's conscious of how they come across to others, and the room is full of people putting on an act, and sizing you up at the same time.

My remedy for this is to get drunk quickly, which reduces my discomfort, and position myself in a corner and throw occasional wisecracks. Today, though, I had Muneeza with me, and I could tell that she was nervous. She hadn't met my friends before, and she had probably never been to a party of this sort. I didn't even know if she drank. I didn't want her to feel awkward and out of place, and if she did, I was prepared to say that I had to rush somewhere else so we could leave early.

'What's with the ponytail, dude?' I asked Ganesh as he opened the door. 'You look like Arindam Chaudhari.'

'I'm already regretting inviting you,' Ganesh said. 'You may leave now, but leave the lady behind please. Hi, I'm Ganesh.'

'Hi, I'm Muneeza.'

'Pleased to meet you, Muneeza. Come on in.'

We walked in and there was a quick round of introductions with the people sitting in the hall, and then Ganesh asked us to help ourselves at the bar. A couple of other guests walked in. We went over to where the drinks were.

'What'll you have, Muneeza?'

'I don't know. What are you having?'

'I'll just have a beer to start with. Do you want one...?'

'Is there Coke?'

'Sure... Here you go.'

We sat ourselves down on the corner of a divan and listened to the conversation. It was about reality shows.

'Look, I don't care what the ratings are, these reality shows are all so crass, yaar,' said Nimisha, a copywriter in the advertising agency where Ganesh worked, patting her spiky red hair.

'I actually like reality shows,' said Monty, a long-haired, bearded assistant director. 'I think reality shows do what great art is supposed to do, only better. See, art is supposed to reveal the human condition. So reality shows do the same thing, only without the artifice.'

'But they're *staged*,' squeaked Nimisha.

'No, yaar, they're not. I have friends who make them, I know.'

'Monty, you're a pseudo, yaar, what human condition?' said a chica I'd never met who was smoking an enormous (and enormously phallic) cigar. 'In all these shows people *know* there's a camera, they're just acting for it.'

'But we know they're acting for it,' said Monty. 'There is no pretence of that. In real life also we act, no, even with ourselves? Everything is a reality show that way – but in a reality show, as opposed to reality, we know what is staged and what is not.'

'Monty, yaar, why're you building an intellectual defence of reality shows, I don't understand,' said Phallic Cigar Chica. 'Next thing you'll be saying Ekta Kapoor is the new Kieślowski or something.'

'No, that's Sanjay Leela Bhansali,' said Monty, and everybody laughed.

Arvind came and sat next to us. Arvind was with Ganesh and me in college, and we used to call him Hyundai Accent because he switches effortlessly between accents without even realizing it. He'd be ideal for a BPO job, I suppose, but he actually works in his father's company in Thane. I'm not sure what the company does – it might even manufacture hydraulic motors. Or pneumatic pumps.

'So, Muneeza,' Arvind asked in an Australian accent. 'Which part of town do you stay in?'

'Lokhandwala.'

'Lokhandwala,' Arvind said in an Irish accent. 'So you stay somewhere close to where Abir stays then. Don't you also stay somewhere there, Abir?'

'That's right.'

'That's wonderful,' said Arvind in an American accent. 'I love how the suburbs are expanding. Lokhandwala has become so cool now, so hip.'

'Yes.'

At this point someone asked Arvind the time, he looked at his watch, and his whisky was all over his shirt. 'Oh panchod,' he said, in a Punjabi accent.

■

Ramona made her entry about half an hour after us. As usual, she looked stunning, the body of the party. She wore a skirt the size of my beer mug and a stylized choli that seemed about 16 sizes too small. A baby could sleep on her cleavage going bouncy bouncy bouncy in bliss, and her nipples were, well, pointy pointy pointy. Dispensing *hellos* and *dahlings* and muas liberally, she bounced her way towards me, leaned down to where I was sitting on the rug, her mammaries swaying pendulously, and kissed my ear. 'Abir, sweeeeetheart, it's been so looong,' she cooed. 'How come I don't seeeee you these days. You haven't got domesticated, have yoooo?'

I glanced at Muneeza. She looked like she was in shock, as if she would pass out any moment, requiring mouth-to-mouth resuscitation that I would generously volunteer to provide. She caught my eye and recovered her composure.

'It's good to see you too, Ramona. Here, meet my friend, Muneeza. Muneeza, Ramona.'

Now Ramona leaned forward and nuzzled against Muneeza's ear. We often call Ramona the Mua Constrictor, though what makes her embrace so overwhelming is not physical force but a combination of her anaesthetic perfume, the speed with which she attacks, and her voluptuosity. She is a force of nature, she is, evolved in prehistoric times with 21st century parties in mind. Who could have thought?

Ramona sat between Muneeza and me, put her hand on my thigh, her nails reaching out halfway across the room, and turned to Muneeza.

'So, Muneeza, you're with Abeeeer?'

Before Muneeza could appreciate the possible import of this question, she'd already answered 'Yes'.

Ramona looked at me, and back at Muneeza. She was toying with us.

'And what do you doooo, Muneeeeza? Are you also a journalist?'

'No, I'm still in college.'

'Still in cawwllege! What are you studying?'

'Um, I'm doing commerce.'

'Cawwmmerce! And what do you plan to do after this?'

'I'm planning to do an MBA.'

'Emm-Bee-Ehhhh! That's wonderful. My brother's doing one at Staaanford. But he says that he wishes he'd gone to New York instead, that's apparently the coolest place to do an Emm-Bee-Ehhh, the big-name colleges are ohhver-rated. Where are you planning to goh?'

'Um, I haven't decided yet.'

'That's the smart thing to dooo! Keep your options open. Excuse me now, I'll go get myself a driiiink.' She pushed down on my thigh for support as she got up, and then swayed across the room towards the bar, all male eyes, and a few resentful female ones as well, on her boooooooty.

I leaned across to Muneeza, 'Don't get put off by Ramona,' I spoke softly into her ear. 'She's a snobby little bitch. Nobody likes her.'

'You seem to be quite a good friend of hers.'

'Don't be silly. She's like that with everyone. Look.' Across the room, Ramona had her arms around the neck of a dude named Abhay, and was moving back and forth, teasing his chest with her mammular charms as she whispered into his ear.

'Is that her boyfriend?' asked Muneeza.

'No, he's gay,' I said. Muneeza shot me a sharp look, and I said, 'No, really, I'm not kidding. He's really gay!'

I tend to wisecrack a lot, because of which I am often not taken seriously. When I was in college, a girl I had the hots for told me that it was impossible to have a conversation with me because I was always dispensing one-liners. I realized later that my wisecracking was a nervous tic. When it came to that particular girl – her name was Roma; all roads led to Roma those days – I was terrified of making a fool of myself by saying something stupid. I was also terrified of saying nothing at all, because I was so nervous that I couldn't think of anything but her lips and her breasts. (Actually, her breasts; I just wrote 'lips' to sound a little respectable.) (I'm kidding.) So I'd wisecrack.

At first it would work, because chicks like guys with a sense of humour. Then they'd get tired of me, because they wanted something besides the bloody sense of humour. Anyway, it did get me further with Roma than any girl before her. We held hands while watching a film in a theatre.

Ruined the film, I'm telling you. But I did feel proud afterwards, as if I was no longer a virgin.

And really, just what is it with these Romas and Ramonas? They'll all be fat aunties by the time life begins for me at 40. Fat aunties in hideous chiffon saris with flower prints. So there.

◾

I graduated to vodka-tonic as the party went on. The music got louder and louder. At one point, Monty tried to dance, tripped on his shoelace and fell on Puneet, another college friend of mine, tearing his shirt and exposing a nipple in the process. How I wish Ramona had been standing there instead. Monty also went on the balcony and puked off its edge — Ganesh's flat was on the fourth floor — and later claimed that an elderly couple on a Luna had had the worst of it. 'Mr Gokhale!' said Ganesh, and we all went silent. But Ganesh didn't seem too worried and the laughter resumed.

Muneeza seemed comfortable enough — the trick at such parties is to find your place in it, and hers, like mine, was in a corner, chilling out without joining too many conversations. Ramona ignored me for the rest of the evening, perhaps feeling that I was taken — and who could argue with that?

◾

'I hope you didn't get bored?' I asked Muneeza as we left the party, at about one in the morning.

'No, of course not,' she said. 'I would have if you weren't there, though.'

'Stunning. Everyone's always said exactly the opposite thing to me.'

I hailed an auto and stumbled while getting into it. I was both sleepy and a little horny – I thought I might need to jerk off before going to sleep.

We arrived home, and I flopped down on the divan and closed my eyes. Then Muneeza sat down beside me.

'Abir, there was something I forgot to tell you today.'

'What?'

'I found out from a friend today that Sonal is coming back to town tomorrow.'

'Oh.'

'So I won't have to bother you anymore.'

'Are you crazy? This is no bother.'

'I know. You've been very kind. But once Sonal is back there is really is no reason for me to stay on here. I thought I'll call her tomorrow evening and then maybe shift day after morning.'

'But there's no reason why you can't stay here! We're both comfortable, aren't we?'

She looked at me, alarmed, and I realized that I was sitting up, all agitated, and I was probably speaking more forcefully than I needed to. Damn you, vodka. I could barely think straight. All I could think was, *No, she'd better not leave now.*

'I'm sorry,' I said. 'No, I mean, I enjoy having you around, but obviously you should do what makes you comfortable. It's just that Sonal probably has a family and so on, and it might be an imposition on them, and I really don't mind.' I was slurring, I think.

Her look had changed to one of concern. 'Abir, it doesn't matter where I stay, you've been a friend to me in a time of need and I'll always be grateful for that.'

'Ya,' I said, and nodded. *I'd better shut up now,* I thought, *I'm probably making a fool of myself. No, I must not say the words forming on my lips...*

'I'm missing you already,' I said.

She smiled and said, 'Goodnight.' Then she touched my arm for just a moment and disappeared into another world. I mean, into the next room. Damn. I was being melodramatic. Damn you, vodka. I should have stuck to orange juice. Or milk.

15. Two Things

When I woke up, she wasn't there. I found a message on the kitchen shelf that said, 'Gone to college, back by four. Didn't want to wake you up. You were sleeping like a baby!' I felt like bawling like a baby.

I simply had to finish the piece now. It was 10.30. I gulped down a cup of coffee, broke my own world record for the fastest bath ever, and rushed to office. I had a mild headache, but I felt lucid and knocked off the piece by two. It began like this:

In July 1987 Mohammad Iqbal married Rehana Iqbal in Dongri. He was 21. She was 19. They barely knew each other – but they knew they wanted to be together. Iqbal, a gaunt, thoughtful young man would tell his daughter Muneeza 15 years later that this was the happiest day of his life. In his wedding photograph, though, he seems to conceal embarrassment rather than joy. He was shy, nervous about what was to come. 'I think I had started loving her even before I knew her,' he told Muneeza. 'Knowing her was just finding that love which was already inside me.' Rehana was dead at the time this conversation happened, and all that the father and daughter could do was look back. And yes, Muneeza says, look forward as well – for she still had her father, and had discovered a kinder, gentler side of him after Rehana Iqbal's death.

But Muneeza is alone today, because her father is also dead.

In July 1987, as Mohammad and Rehana stood facing each other, a teenager named Vallabh Thombre was sprinting to meet his father a few blocks away. Vallabh was in school when his friend, Santya, got a message that his mother was unwell. The boys ran home and took her to the hospital. She was breathless, clutching her chest. Maybe she was in the middle of a heart attack; Vallabh doesn't remember now. He does remember that the hospital ignored them, and made them wait, and asked them to 'drink water'. Vallabh then ran to the nearby police station, where his father was an inspector. His father came to the hospital with him, and Santya's mother became a VIP patient. On that day, Vallabh decided that he would join the police when he grew up.

The rhythm of Bombay is relentless: in one ear I hear the excited heartbeat of Mohammad Iqbal looking at the woman he is marrying; in the other the sound of Vallabh Thombre running towards his future, his feet beating down on the tar road with the inevitability of destiny. Last month, one of these sounds cancelled the other out.

After this I mentioned the shootout, and then I wrote about the men separately, wrapping it all together in the end. My story painted Iqbal as a good man screwed by circumstance; but it showed Thombre as a creature of circumstance as well. My portraits of both men were sympathetic.

I took a printout and left it in Sandhya's cabin, as she'd asked me to. I liked the story I had written, even if some of it was overwrought (*the inevitability of destiny*; huh?). I deliberately overwrote it a bit because it's exactly those 'poetic' touches that people like Sandhya tend to like.

And now I headed out for lunch, thinking about the bigger problem that I faced: Muneeza. My friend, Sancho.

In just a day, she would leave my house. No doubt I'd still meet her after that, but we'd both have to go out of our way, and I'd have to find an excuse to do so. I had known for a while, I suppose, what I needed to do next. But now I had a deadline. What an ironic trick for life to play on a journalist.

I didn't want to go up to her in a romantic moment and tell her that I cared for her. That was obvious – and any relationship that grew out of such a confession would be based on dishonesty if I didn't clear up a few other things first.

There were two things I needed to tell her: One, I needed her to know that I knew Vallabh Thombre well, and that I had been there when her father was killed, outside the building, that I had heard her scream, that I had worried more about my awkward situation than the sorrow of the girl inside. Two, I needed to tell her about this story I had written, which showed Thombre to be a flawed (understandably flawed) human being rather than a communal, heartless murderer.

The first of these she would never know if I didn't tell her. But I had to tell her, or our relationship would be founded on the lie of a truth not revealed. The first time our lives crossed was not when I saw her leaving Mahesh's room with Meenakshi, but on the night I heard her scream. I would not be able to come to terms with it unless she did first. And surely she would understand: I was just doing my job; I didn't know her then; I didn't know what was happening.

Also, I didn't want her to read my story before I could tell her about it. She might like the parts about her father (and her), but she would certainly consider everything I had written about Thombre to be a betrayal. Her father had been killed, and in her eyes, I could either be for her or against her, against Thombre or for Thombre. There were no nuances here, no shades of grey.

Of course, Thombre would not have been part of the story if Sandhya hadn't insisted on it. But I couldn't pass the buck, I had to take responsibility. And I really did believe that Thombre was not a cold-hearted murderer. I hated the system he was part of, the system that we are all a part of — but in his place, born in his family, brought up as he was, would I have made different choices? Perhaps not.

I bought myself my regular tuna sandwich at Subway, but couldn't finish it. For some reason, I was repulsed by the tuna. I got myself a black coffee. I looked at all the people around me, all of whom, without exception, had surely faced greater emotional turbulence than this, and made harder choices. And yet here we all were, engrossed in normalness, like I would be one day as well, when all this would seem trivial. I would also, like the guy at the next table, be the proud owner of a substantial paunch and a double chin, with a wife and two kids by my side. And I would feel happy, regardless of whether that woman answered to the name of Sancho or not. So happy, so foolishly happy.

◾

'I spoke to Sonal, she told me to come today only, but I said I'll come tomorrow.'

'Oh, okay. I'll drop you if you want.'

'You don't have to. I'm sure you must have work. How's the story going?'

'I finished it.'

'Oh! Can I see it?'

'Er, it's just a first draft. I'd rather let my editor see it and then I'll show you the final draft. Listen...'

'What?'

'We need to talk. There are two things I need to tell you.'

'Two?' she said, as if this was one more than she was expecting.

'Yes,' I said. 'Two things. Sit.'

She sat. She knew from my expression, I suppose, that I was worried by what I needed to say. She didn't seem so worried. What could I possibly say that would worry her? At most I would confess about past relationships, girls I had had sex with, girls like Ramona maybe. That didn't bother her.

'The last two years in this newspaper, you know that I've been on the crime beat, right?'

'Yes.'

'Well, my job involved being friends with policemen, using them as contacts and so on. Often they would call me after an arrest and I would do a story on the case they had cracked. They would brief me, informally, about the progress they were making on investigations they were doing.'

'Hmm.'

'Well, one of the cops I know well, his name is Vallabh Thombre.' Muneeza's face froze when I said his name. 'He would call me often and brief me about cases.' I paused here. I didn't know how to go on.

'And?'

'And, well, one evening when I was in office, he called me and asked if I wanted to accompany him and his team for a routine arrest they were making. He said he had received a tipoff about some gangsters staying in a building in Mahalaxmi. He said his men would arrest them, and I could report the arrest. I thought, it's a routine story, not very different from the stories I do. I mean, this is my work. So I went along with him.'

I paused to catch my breath. She waited.

'So we got to this address, and Thombre asked me to wait outside. So I waited outside. Then I heard gunshots, and I realized that something had gone wrong. Then Thombre came out and told me that they had killed a gangster who opened fire on them, and I should file a report to that effect.'

She realized now. She opened her mouth; her lips trembled; but she didn't say anything.

'I was just doing my job, Muneeza. I didn't know anything else. I just went and filed my report.'

'You... Are you saying you were there that night?'

'I was outside.'

'You were there when they killed my father?'

She got up now. Her voice was beginning to betray all the stress of the past two weeks.

'I was outside, Muneeza. I was just doing my job. I thought it was a routine arrest. It could have been any other crime reporter.'

I was panicking now. My mind was blank. I had planned my defence, but I forgot the words now. I would not be able to eloquently persuade her, as I had planned. She was not the only person lost in her emotion.

'But my father was not a gangster!' She was half-shouting, half-crying now.

'I know that now. I didn't know that then.'

'You're a journalist. You were there. You should have written about it. Those murderers would have been in jail then!'

'But I didn't know what had happened. What could I write about?'

'What do you mean you didn't know? You knew. You were there. Don't lie to me. Of course you knew. You knew and you walked away. After they killed my father.'

'Listen, Muneeza...'

'Don't call me that! Don't take my name! You're just like them then. You're no different. You're also a murderer. You were there.'

'Muneeza, be calm...' I reached out to touch her; she pushed me away.

'Don't touch me. You bastard! You should have exposed them. You're a journalist. That's your duty!'

'Muneeza, it's not so simple, they would just have denied it, I'd have had no proof, it wouldn't have been credible.'

'Why didn't you tell me this earlier? Why? Why?'

'Muneeza, how could I...'

'And why're you telling me this now?'

'I'm sorry I didn't tell you this. I'm just trying to be honest now...'

'What honest? Huh, what honest? Answer one question, Abir, answer one question: do you believe my father was a gangster?'

'No, no, of course not!'

'Then why couldn't you be honest and expose his murderers? Why?'

I had nothing to say to that. I just stood and looked at her dumbstruck. She was crying. My brain was in meltdown.

'What was the second thing you wanted to tell me?'

I remembered that other thing; but how could I tell her? I couldn't think, so I said the only thing that I was sure of now, the only thing that made any sense.

'I've fallen in love with you.'

There was a moment's silence that I'll always remember, and a look she gave me that was worse than a slap. Then she walked into her room, shut the door, and latched it. I could hear her throw her bag on the bed. I knew she was packing. I knew she was leaving. I didn't know what to do. Nothing I could say was persuasive now, even to me. She was right – I was a coward. What meaning did my falling in love with her have, then, if this is what I was?

She didn't look at me as she left, just marched straight out and banged the door shut behind her. I didn't try to stop her or say anything. I sat on the floor with my head in my hands. Then I curled up on the divan and cried.

What could I have done differently? Well, really, nothing. Trying to do an exposé on the death of her father when it had happened would have been an act of foolish and pointless bravado – and I hadn't even known then that he was an innocent man. Things like that happen in Bombay every day. Big injustices, little omissions, on the streets and in our lives. Mostly you have to let them pass, and concentrate on the stuff that you can control, on the things that matter.

Now it mattered, of course – but now it was too late. Now I would do anything for her – but there was nothing I could do. All that mattered was what had already happened, and I didn't have a time machine. I could only go forward.

16. The Bat's-Eye View

After Muneeza left I thought I wouldn't be able to sleep, and would stay up all night, worrying for her and grieving for me. I went and got myself a can of beer. I sat on the divan and played with my phone. She didn't have a mobile phone, this girl I hadn't known until just a few days ago, and now she was out of reach. If she'd had one, of course, she wouldn't have picked it up now if I called. But I could have sent her messages. Desperate, sentimental messages that she would save and show our children one day as she said, *See, your daddy was a softy.*

Softy my ass, a little one would yell back. *Tell him to shave before he gives me kissie. That chin of his is no softy.*

Oh fuck fuck fuck fuck fuck.

I held my head in my hands. Then I lay down, and practised my Devdas look. I thought I would never be able to sleep again, never ever – but as soon as the thought came to me, I felt terribly tired and closed my eyes.

◾

I woke up early, maybe around seven or so. I hugged my pillow and smiled, as if all was well with the world and there was someone sleeping in the next room. Then I realized that the light was on, and I remembered what had happened the previous evening.

I got up with a start. My mobile phone, waiting patiently besides me to ring the alarm, took one look at me and trotted off to the corner to sulk. A pigeon landed on the windowsill and looked at me disapprovingly. I looked back. I blinked first.

My first thought was that I needed to find out if Muneeza had reached Sonal's house safely. Bombay is normally a safe city for women, and the journey to Thane at that time of night wouldn't have been a sweat. But I needed to find out — and I wanted to hear her voice. Sonal's number was saved on my phone, and I decided I would call her after nine, which seemed a decent time to call.

But what would I say to Muneeza?

All the arguments I'd carefully prepared came back to me now. I thought that once she got over the shock of what I'd told her, she would understand.

She had, after all, begun to like me in these last few days. She would give me the benefit of the doubt once I managed to speak to her. She would be my friend again, and we would go to Eterniti, have black coffee and iced tea, and make a fresh start.

Or would she? How could I be so sure? Was this just wishful thinking?

When I was in college, I would often bore my friends by talking about an essay I loved by Thomas Nagel called 'What Is It Like to Be a Bat?' Nagel's basic point in the essay is that some kinds of experience are beyond human understanding, an assertion he illustrates by talking about bats. Bats don't have eyes – they navigate the world using something called echolocation. They emit high-frequency sounds, and form a 'visual' map of the world around them by the reflections of these sounds. That is how, to put it crudely, they 'see'.

Nagel says that the nature of that experience is so different from anything we know that we cannot even imagine it. He stresses that even if he could somehow imagine how it would be for *him* to be a bat, he couldn't possibly imagine how it would be for a *bat* to be a bat.

And how was it for Muneeza to be Muneeza?

Oh, I could put myself in her shoes and rationally figure out how she must be feeling right now, and what she felt for me, and so on. But all this was just my vanity. It was me being Muneeza – and it was a futile effort because I wasn't equipped for that task. I hadn't lived her life. I hadn't lost her mother so young, or even known her. I hadn't seen her father die in front of me from a gunshot wound, with a posse of uniformed men looking on callously. Most pertinently, from my point of view, I hadn't met this glib, wisecracking young man from a privileged background who feigned such friendship, and pretended to care, even as he deceived her. This flippant young fool who had no way of understanding the depth of her grief, but arrogantly pretended to sympathize.

So how could she trust this boy who was, after all, someone she had met just a few days ago? What did he know of her that he could say, so stupidly, that he had fallen in love with her?

■

It wasn't only Muneeza who was a stranger to me – I, too, felt like a stranger to myself. If I had to sit down and think about what I was doing and why I was doing it, I would have no answers. Why did I start feeling so strongly for this girl? Was it because I was at a stage in life when I needed companionship (or romance or sex), and fell for the first girl who did not threaten my self-image? Was I attracted to her because she was vulnerable and aroused my protective instincts? Whatever it was in her that I had fallen in love with, was it so unique that no one else had it? If I had met her in different circumstances, say if we bumped into each other at Bookends while browsing through books, would I have looked at her twice?

Questions, questions. If only some part of me could pop up and press the buzzer. But alas, I had no answers.

The clock struck nine. I dialled Sonal's number. The phone rang five times, a matter to which various interpretations could be attached. Then a girl answered.

'Hi, is that Sonal?' I said.

'Yes.'

'Hi. I'm sorry to disturb you, I'm Abir Ganguly, Muneeza's friend. Muneeza left for your place last night, and I just wanted to make sure that she arrived safely.'

'Oh. Yes, she did, she arrived safely.'

'May I speak to her?'

'Of course. Just a moment.'

Clearly Muneeza hadn't told Sonal any of what had happened. I heard a murmuring in the background, and then, after an interval of about 20 seconds, Sonal came back on the line.

'Er, I'm sorry, but Muneeza doesn't want to speak to you.'

'Oh.'

I heard *her* voice, very faint, in the background. Then Sonal:

'And, er, she says she doesn't want you to call again.'

'Okay... Thank you.'

I had a cup of coffee, showered, and headed to office. I had handed in my article, and now it was back to the grind. Also, I needed company. I would go mad on my own, listening to the bewildered babble in my head.

I went to my cubicle and switched on my computer. I tapped my fingers on my desk as it booted. I picked up a copy of the previous day's *Afternoon Mail* lying on the neighbouring desk and browsed through it. The Afternoon Hottie on page 3, in a green bikini, looked like she wanted a brownie desperately, with ice cream. The columnist TV Iyengar had a piece on the edit page about how the government was failing the citizens of Mumbai, and only government intervention could solve the problem. Our cricket captain was saying on the sports page that the boys played well, but the boys in the opposing team played better. Bollywood stars and TV starlets played musical chairs on the gossip page. And some bastard who should have been strangled at birth had filled up the sudoku.

I went online. There was nothing there. Every page was blank.

'The broadband is down,' said D'Souza, who had crept up behind me, a chopper in hand. (Okay, no chopper.) 'It should be back in half an hour, I'm told.'

I looked up at him. His expression changed to one of concern.

'Is everything okay?'

I suppose my eyes were red. 'I've got conjunctivitis,' I said.

Realizing he had caught me in a private moment, he turned to go. Then he paused, and said, 'Well, you take care. I had conjunctivitis once at your age. It didn't last long.'

◾

Damle, one of the office peons, came and told me that Sandhya Madam wanted to see me in her cabin.

'Abir, I just read your piece, it's really good, well done.'

'Thanks. I'm glad you liked it.'

'I thought I should tell you, though, that the launch of *The Mumbaikar* has been delayed. There are some sponsorship issues. Economic downturn and all, you know.'

'Oh. So when is it scheduled to launch now?'

'Well, I just chatted with Mahesh, and we're not quite sure. We have enough content now to fill up a dummy issue, but we're not going to work on any more till the picture becomes clearer. I'm going to look after the Sunday supplement until we sort that out. Mahesh has spoken to D'Souza, who says he'll be glad to have you back on the crime beat.'

'Ah. Okay.'

'But I hope we print this story someday, Abir. It's a very well-done story, and I'm very impressed by how deep you went into all the characters, and how much empathy you've shown in it. Well done.'

'Characters'. 'Empathy'. 'Deep'. Condescending female dog!

∎

So it was back to square one here as well. The crime beat looked so different now from a couple of weeks ago. When I went out to do stories in the future, would I still be so cynical? Earlier, when I reported on a crime or an event, I'd treat the people

I wrote about as mere characters in a story for me –
and not quite real people. Would I still do that?

Would I still look for a mosquito stain on a dead
man's shirt?

I checked if our broadband connection was
working, so that I could surf the web a bit for
distraction. I typed in www.indiauncut.com and
pressed 'enter'. Nada. Problem loading page, server
not found. In my melodramatic state of mind, this
seemed apt. It felt like the internet would always be
down, and all lines of communication would remain
closed.

Just then, the phone rang.

It was my mother. 'Shona, this is Ma. I just called
to say that I'm arriving tomorrow morning by the
Kingfisher flight. What are you doing tomorrow?'

'Er, nothing much, I can take an off if you
want.'

'No, no need to take an off. I have meetings
all day and a flight to Amsterdam late at night. I
thought I will come to your house, drop my bags,
and then go for my meetings. And then we'll have
dinner before I leave.'

'Sure. But why do you need to drop your
bags?'

'I don't want to make the company book a hotel room when I'm not staying the night, and I don't want to leave my bags in the car. The driver I use in Bombay is very absent-minded.'

'Hmm.'

'And can you message me your address? I don't remember the way, and this driver has never been to your house, as far as I remember.'

'Sure, I'll do that. What time does your flight land?'

'Nine-ish.'

'I'll come and receive you at the airport.'

'Don't be silly, Abir, you don't need to do that.'

'No, I'll come.'

'You sound very tired, Abir. Is everything okay? Are you having your meals on time?'

'Yes, Ma.'

Pause.

'Ma, there was something I wanted to talk to you about.'

'Oh. Okay. Is it something important?'

'Ya. I'll tell you tomorrow.'

'Okay, shona. Bye, now.'

'Bye.'

Why did I say I'd pick up my mother at the airport during a routine visit of hers? And why did I want to speak to her about this?

Well, I had to speak to *someone*. Maybe talking things through would help bring some clarity to the situation.

◾

Mohan came over to my desk. He had a grin on his face that went all the way around his head, and if it was any deeper he would have decapitated himself.

'Hey, dude,' I said. 'What are you so happy about?'

'I have something to show you.'

'What?'

He rested an elbow on the table. 'Feel my bicep.'

17. Precious Things

My mother smiled as she emerged from the airport, and got straight down to business. 'Ah, there you are, shona, my strong son,' she said, kissing my forehead as everyone around laughed openly at me and took pictures of us. 'Take my bags, will you, you're a man now.'

'I was always a man,' I told her. 'I mean, I've always volunteered to carry your bags. What does manhood have to do with it?'

'Nothing, shona, nothing,' she said. 'Lokkhi chhele! Where is my car? Ah, there is my driver.'

A dude who looked like Keshto Mukherjee came towards us and grabbed the handle of a suitcase I was pulling. 'Hello, madam, hello, sir,' he said. 'Good morning!'

'Good morning, Datta,' said my mother. 'Let us go.'

At this point Datta just stood there and looked at us, utterly perplexed by this strange instruction.

'So what did you want to talk to me about, Abir?'

We were in the car, we'd finished off some small talk, and Datta the Doofus Driver was sitting in front, listening to every word.

'Er, I'll tell you later, Ma, when we're in the flat.'

'Is this regarding that girlfriend of yours, that Sanju?'

'Ma, she's not my girlfriend. She's not even my friend now. We had a fight.'

'Oh.' There was a moment of silence as she contemplated the import of this.

'What did you fight about?'

'Well, it's sort of complicated.'

'And you like this girl?'

'Ya. I suppose so.' I felt madly embarrassed, and regretted having even considered talking to my mother about this. 'But it's not just about my liking someone, is it?'

'Don't worry, shona, everything will work out. Even I didn't like your Baba to begin with. But he was persistent, and see what came out of it.'

We flashed each other wry smiles. In the front seat, meanwhile, Datta wasn't smiling – he just looked confused, even worried. Was it the traffic, or his concern for young lovers? We were approaching home, and Datta piped up in a sing-song voice. 'Where from here?' he said. 'Left or right?'

We had to take the next left turn, which was about 100 metres ahead, so I said left. The dude swerved left immediately, into a housing complex called Park Towers. My mother slapped her forehead. Datta, realizing too late that he had made a mistake, smiled sheepishly. 'I thought, left,' he said – and who could fault the poor man?

Quiz question: If you were driving towers instead of cars, and you needed a place to park them, what instruction would you look for?

Okay, forget I even said that.

We got home, and Datta and I carried up the bags. She asked him to wait by the car for half an hour, and went for a quick shower. I was worried that Muneeza might have left a bra inside, and my mother would emerge holding up the bra as if it was a disgusting dead rat that had found its way into her purse.

'Look what I found, Abir,' she would say. 'It appears to be a bra. In *your* bathroom. And what is more, it is a *Muslim* bra. Explain yourself.'

But nothing of the sort happened. She emerged from her shower, and spoke into her mobile phone to a colleague in a brisk, business-like manner. (*I am really curious to know the basis for your rather optimistic projections, Rajeev.*) Then she left.

'I'll try to be back by eight,' she said, 'so that we can finish with dinner by 10, and then I will go to the airport. Is that alright?'

'Ya. I'll make sure I'm back here by eight.'

'Good. Bye now, and sorry that I'm getting late, I can't sit and talk with you now. We'll chat about Sanju in the evening, promise, at length. How long have you known her?'

If I answered that question honestly, my mother would probably fall to the floor guffawing, and roll around there for half an hour.

'Er, not very long, we met earlier this year.'

'Okay, shona, bye now, take care.' She patted me on the head and left.

⬛

I had a bath and went out for lunch by myself. I didn't need to go to work today – the whole Muneeza business was messing with my head, and D'Souza, that kind, genial man with a heart of 44-carat gold, had told me that I could take a couple of days off, and rejoin his department on Thursday. I had two days to sort out Love – and then I could spend the rest of my days on Crime.

I went to Eterniti and got myself a sandwich at Subway. Normally I read while eating alone, but I felt unable to focus today, and looked around me blankly. For months I had been used to eating here on my own – and had enjoyed it that way. Then suddenly I met this girl, and came here with her a couple of times. Now my solitude was accompanied by loneliness, all because of this accidental meeting.

If I was to read a book in which all this had happened, I would be struck by the improbability of the encounter that started this off. But then, if you think about it, everything is improbable. Humans as a species would not exist if not for extremely improbable things happening consistently over millennia. I would not exist if my parents hadn't felt horny at just the moment they did, or if the phone had rung while they were at it. We are all products of accidental events – and after they happen, we look back at them as if they were inevitable, constructing narratives where none exist.

We meet someone at a party we may not have gone to, fall in love, and later decide that this was meant to be, and we were made for each other. We take one job instead of another, do well in an unexpected assignment, and find ourselves in another continent after two years – while in a parallel universe our mirror self, who accepted that other job, gets laid off because of the recession. None of this is destiny – most of this is luck. Things happen, and decisions we make that seem small at the time later turn out to be life-changing.

Two weeks ago my life was clay, and I could make of it what I wanted; but now it had been moulded, and given this shape. To deny it, or to try changing it back, would involve the breaking of things – precious things.

◾

I returned home and thought about the different endings of this story.

Ending One: I call Sonal, and Muneeza agrees to speak to me. She is hesitant, and I have to do a lot of convincing before she agrees to meet me. But I know my battle is won then, and I take her to Eterniti, where we have shared memories. We become friends; and very soon, we become romantically involved. She gets over her father's death, and we spend many happy moments in my flat on afternoons like this, me sitting on the divan, she lying down with her head on my lap, as music plays in the background. A tranquil scene.

'Can't you play something softer?' she says. 'Something more romantic.'

'You don't like Metallica?' I ask, astonished.

Ending Two: I call Sonal, Muneeza comes on the line, and tells me to get out of her life and leave her alone. She tells me that she hates me, and she tells me why, and I realize that she has a point. The harshness in her voice, and her intransigence, leads me to the conclusion that I don't actually like her so much myself, and am better off without her. (I'm rationalizing already.) I get over her, and acquire a drop-dead gorgeous girlfriend in the coming months, who is an heiress, and who Ramona begs for beauty tips.

'How do you look so beee-yooootiful?' Ramona asks her.

'My love for Abir makes me glow,' she says. 'And he's so very good in bed.'

Ending Three: I call Sonal, Muneeza doesn't come on the line. I go to her college to stake her out, but I can't catch a glimpse of her. One day when I do, she looks different — thinner, paler, her unhappiness sketched permanently into her now-bony face. I talk to her, but she is cold, and there is no chemistry. I go away, but I always love the Muneeza I used to know, and remember her fondly as my first love for the rest of my life. I wish her well, and I hope she has found happiness in life — somewhere, somehow.

All of my three endings had one thing in common: 'I call Sonal.' I knew I wasn't going to give this up. Endings Two and Three were possible – but I would bloody well not let them happen. Suddenly, I realized that I didn't face a dilemma at all. There was only one thing I could do.

And what about unloading my heart to my mother, and asking her for advice? I realized it was silly, and I didn't need to do that. Like many people who seek advice, I already knew the answers I needed. If she told me that I should forget about Muneeza, and allow her to introduce me to some nice Bengali girls, like Kavery the daughter of that nice Mr Chatterjee of the Tatas, would I listen to her? No freaking way.

In any case, my mother was late, and missed dinner with me. She called me at seven and said, 'Shona, I'm leaving in 15 minutes, I should be at your house an hour after that, and then we can go out for a quick dinner.'

'Where are you right now?'

'I'm at our Nariman Point office. Bye now.'

She expected to get from Nariman Point to Andheri, by road, in an hour? I felt like saying: *I*

am really curious to know the basis for your rather
optimistic projections, Ma.

◼

I sat on my divan with my phone in my hand,
my heart pumping furiously with a disco beat
that Mithunda could have danced to all night. I
scrolled down to Sonal's number. I pressed the green
button.

'Hello?'

'Hi. Is that Sonal?'

'Yes.'

'Sonal, hi, this is Abir Ganguly. Muneeza's friend.
May I speak to Muneeza?'

She paused — and then she said, softly, 'Just a
minute.'

For a moment, I could not believe this. This meant
that Muneeza was willing to speak to me — otherwise
she would have told Sonal not to pass on any calls
from me. She must have chatted with Sonal about
this — and she must have decided, at the end of it,
that she would talk to me, and allow me to hear her
voice again. But what would she say?

'You sentimental fool,' I suddenly heard a voice
say — and it wasn't coming from the phone. The
lizard sat on the wall, eyeing me warily.

'What's your problem now?' I asked.

'What's my problem?' repeated the lizard mockingly. 'My problem, Abir, is that you are no longer the Abir Ganguly I thought I knew. I was so happy when that girl left, I thought I could have you to myself now. But you're no longer the boy I fell in love with.'

'Fell in love with? Dude, you're just a lizard!'

'Yes, that's what you say now. But it wasn't always like this.'

'What're you talking about? You were always a lizard. We just banter, we never had a relationship.'

'Well, okay, it hadn't got physical yet, I'll grant you that. But we were more than friends, and I was just waiting for you to take it to another level. But now you've gone and fallen in love with this, this, *girl*. How could you?'

'Well, things happen, you know. And I hate to break your heart, but I never had feelings for you. It would never have worked out.'

'Yes,' said the lizard. 'I can see that now. I'm just a lizard, and that's not good enough for you. Well, fine, do what you must. But I promise to jump on her in the middle of the night every night. Soon she will realize it's not working, and she will go away again.'

'You're getting ahead of yourself here. She may never come back here, or be my friend again. She may tell me now to get out of her life forever.'

'I wish. But somehow, I have a feeling that won't happen. Lizards sense these things, you know.'

'Hmm,' I said.

Just then I heard Sonal's distant voice say something on the other side of the phone. I heard the phone shift hands. And Muneeza came on the line and said, 'Hello?'

Acknowledgments

Nilanjana S. Roy and Sonia Faleiro read first drafts of this book, and their enthusiasm and advice were invaluable.

Krishna Warrier, Nyela Saeed, Prem Panicker and Vikram Sathaye patiently answered my questions and gave me much insight while I was doing my research. I'm grateful for their time.

My parents, Keshav and Jaya Varma, gave me the freedom and space to be whatever I wanted. Little did they know it would come to this.

Jasmine Shah Varma commented on this book as it developed, drowned its writer in coffee, and indulged the foolishness you have before you. This book may not have existed without her, so if you don't like it, it's her fault. So there.